OUTLAWS OF THE BIG BEND

OUTLAWS OF
THE BIG BEND

JACKSON COLE

WHEELER
CHIVERS

This Large Print edition is published by Wheeler Publishing, Waterville, Maine, USA and by BBC Audiobooks Ltd, Bath, England.
Wheeler Publishing, a part of Gale, Cengage Learning.
Wheeler Publishing Large Print Western.
The text of this Large Print edition is unabridged.
Other aspects of the book may vary from the original edition.
Set in 16 pt. Plantin.
Printed on permanent paper.

LIBRARY OF CONGRESS CATALOGING-IN-PUBLICATION DATA
Cole, Jackson.
Outlaws of the Big Bend / by Jackson Cole.
p. cm. — (Wheeler Publishing large print western)
ISBN-13: 978-1-59722-907-4 (pbk. : alk. paper)
ISBN-10: 1-59722-907-5 (pbk. : alk. paper)
1. Outlaws—Fiction. 2. Large type books. I. Title.
PS3505.O2685O98 2009
813'.52—dc22   2008045598

BRITISH LIBRARY CATALOGUING-IN-PUBLICATION DATA AVAILABLE

Published in 2009 in the U.S. by arrangement with Golden West Literary Agency.
Published in 2009 in the U.K. by arrangement with Golden West Literary Agency.

U.K. Hardcover: 978 1 408 43268 6 (Chivers Large Print)
U.K. Softcover: 978 1 408 43269 3 (Camden Large Print)

Printed in the United States of America
2 3 4 5 6   13 12 11 10 09
ED285

Outlaws of the Big Bend

Chapter I
Killers in
Sombreros

When outlaws of the Big Bend organize for plunder, it's up to the Lone Wolf Lawman to smash their grim schemes and to disband their closely-knit, sinister fellowship of murder!

The night wind howled across the wild reaches of the Big Bend, a land so vast it was a universe in itself. Only the huge state of Texas could lose within its borders such a large, sparsely inhabited area.

There was a moon, but dark clouds kept scudding across its yellow face, cutting off the light. As the clouds passed, the moon shone again, so that the land was no longer lost in shadowy blackness.

The riders who traversed it were headed north on a winding trail over rolling grasslands between the mountains. This was range on which cattle and other stock could subsist. To the south loomed the fabulous

Chisos Mountains, where outlaw Apaches and other fugitives lurked in unexplored fastnesses. And beyond the Chisos lay the Rio Grande, which for miles ran through a deep-cut canyon separating the United States from Mexico, with only a pass or two which men and animals could negotiate.

As the moonlight was unshuttered once more, it touched dark faces and glinting eyes. It hovered over high-peaked sombreros that were pulled low and chin-straps drawn taut to foil the whipping wind, while black cloaks and capes were well-wrapped about the riders' bodies.

There were fifty to sixty following a leader who, even in that sinister array, stood out. He was a big fellow, with an almost black face and a heavy beard with upcurving sideburns. A Mexican hat trimmed with rows of silver buttons and from beneath which tangled black hair escaped, was cocked at a jaunty angle on his head. His bulky body was clad in black leather. He wore black chaps, and his blue jacket was buttoned to the throat, where a bandanna cradled his jowls.

The plodding riders were silent, intent on reaching their goal. Leather creaked, while now and then came a faint metallic click as a gun-barrel touched a metal stirrup.

Two of the riders whose faces were unmasked as were the faces of the others in the cavalcade, came spurring back and signaled the burly chief. With his arms, the leader urged his men on. They came over a rise and could look down into a natural basin in which a small fire glowed, the embers reddened in the draught. Against the light could be seen several figures and nearby were cattle, a bunch which had been collected and which the cowboys were guarding.

The leader of the sinister dark-clad riders pulled up his bandanna, and his men did likewise.

They fanned out an attack as their carbines and shotguns rose. They gave no warning but opened fire as they swept in. It was a vicious, unprovoked assault.

One of the cowboys by the fire died as he turned toward the onrushing men. Another screamed and fell, his side ripped by buckshot. The horses of the cowboys guarding the cattle were standing some yards away, but only one of the men with the herd managed to reach a mount and spur away through the spreading lines of rustlers.

The big steers were pawing the ground snorting and bawling restlessly, for the sound of the fight had excited them. Expert handlers among the attackers started them moving south, and the killers, letting the victims lie in their own blood, turned back, running the cows before them.

Lightning blazed across the sky, and thunder pealed. The steers ran madly on. The moon was lost behind a rolling black cloud, and big raindrops pattered down as the storm came, suddenly and fiercely, beating upon the Big Bend. The heavens seemed to open and pour out millions of tons of water, water which flattened the loose sandy soil and cut new little channels as it ran off the higher spots. . . .

The stormy night passed at last, and the gray dawn came. Soon after the sun rose, young Jerry Addison, bronco buster and mustanger for the KO Ranch in Big Bend, so named because "K. O." were the first two initials of the owner, rode into the ranch-yard and dismounted. He was returning from a trip to select a spot that could be used as a trap for wild horses.

One glance at the sober faces of the men in the yard and lounging in the bunkhouse door showed him that something was seriously wrong. He walked over to K. O. Pierce, the rancher with whom he had a temporary job breaking the mustangs brought in from the hills. They were often

as wild as if they'd never seen a human being.

The look on the rancher's face only in-
creased Jerry Addison's uneasiness. Kenneth
Osmond Pierce looked as though the entire
world had rolled on him, and he felt its
entire weight. A sad expression was on his
wind reddened face, and his wide mouth
was grim. In his light-blue eyes was deep
misery.

"What's wrong, K. O.?" Jerry asked anxiously. Knowing Pierce as he did, how well
everyone liked the rancher, how much his
men respected him, and would even be willing to die for him, if need be, he also knew
that it must have been stark tragedy that
had struck the big, bearded Texan.

It was.

"Rustlers shot and killed my brother Ed
last night, Addison," Pierce told him, his
voice husky and choked. "They got Shorty
Lewis, too. He was about gone when we
found him lyin' in the mud and rainwater.
Shorty died while we were bringin' him
home. Two more of my boys got hit by
rustler lead. Art Green was the only one of
the five watchin' them cows who come
home all in one piece!"

Addison gripped the rancher's hand in
sympathy. "Them rustlers got some nerve,

K. O.," he said then. "How many were there?"

"Well, Art and the others who can talk claim there must've been hunderds," Pierce told him, "but allowin' for the excitement and the dark, yuh can prob'ly shave that down to sixty or seventy. They were Mexicans, they say, Chihuahua Pete's gang. This Chihuahua Pete's a huge hombre, come from below the Border, I reckon. He's gettin' active in these parts. We're goin' after 'em now."

"I'll saddle Blue and be ready when yuh start," Jerry said promptly.

"Obliged boy," said Pierce. "It ain't in yore contract to fight, but we'll be mighty glad to have yuh."

Pierce turned away, his big shoulders drooped. He was crushed by the death of his younger brother and the loss of his friend "Shorty."

Pierce was a man of fifty, whose temples were touched with gray. Right now, he wore spurred boots, a red star at their tops, and into which corduroys were tucked, a brown shirt, and a large Stetson with a curving brim.

He and his men had been out in the night, to bring in the wounded after the alarm had reached the ranchhouse. With the new day,

12

they were making ready to ride on the trail of Chihuahua Pete and his killers.

Jerry Addison himself was under twenty-five, of medium height and with a wiry body. His muscles were well-developed, for his work as a bronc buster required an acrobat's build and nerve. His crisp hair had a reddish tinge, and his fair complexion was sprinkled with freckles. His features were pleasant, his eyes large, and deep-blue. His slim figure looked well in his leather shirt with its rawhide lacing, leather riding pants, and half-boots. The brim of his Stetson was not so wide as the usual cowboy headgear.

Everybody called him "Jerry" or "Addison." He never confessed that he had been christened "Jeremiah," for young as he was he feared the boys would have ragged him unmercifully over such a fancy name.

When he walked toward the low bunkhouse it was with a rather stiff-legged gait, caused by the high heels on his riding boots and his erect carriage. Jerry Addison was not a regular member of the KO outfit, though Pierce hired about twenty men in season. But the rancher owned a good many horses which were turned out on the range, and every year he needed an expert such as Addison to break new ones in so his cowboys could handle them.

Sometimes one ride by the bronc buster was all that was needed to bring a horse down to the level where the average cowboy could use the animal. Others had to be saddled and run several times, while occasionally a bad specimen could not be made use of at all.

It was Addison's life, to travel from one ranch to another, spending a week or two at each, or whatever time was required to gentle the mustangs on hand. He liked the work. It was interesting and exciting, and provided plenty of change from the usual ranch routine. The pay was better, too, than a cowboy earned. In between jobs, he could spend time in the towns, or take a run somewhere to hunt and fish. It brought prestige, for in the cattle country a top rider was respected and looked up to.

Pierce's ranch, in the heart of the Big Bend country, was unfenced range, covered by sparse bunch grasses on which the cattle could subsist by constant roaming in the hunt for food. The house, built of adobe bricks and of one story like the other buildings, stood on high ground above the bank of a brown-watered river which flowed southeast and eventually, through a deep, narrow side canyon, joined the Rio Grande.

This stream formed the chief water supply for the ranch and for the animals, although there were a few water-holes farther out, within reach of Pierce's steers.

Since the range was open, the cattle of other ranchers, Pierce's neighbors, mingled with the KO herds.

As Jerry Addison reached the bunkhouse, to prepare to go along on the rustler hunt, Pierce's men were at the horse corrals, roping and saddling their horses. All had strapped on gun-belts, and gleaming carbines stood against the fence rails, waiting to be picked up.

Jerry Addison buckled on his own cartridge belt, and checked his walnut-stocked six-shooter before dropping it back into the holster. He owned a fine Winchester hunting rifle, and decided to take it for long-range work in case they sighted the cow thieves. This had a special leather case and attachment loop so it could be carried under his leg when he rode.

He brought out his good saddle, an expensive job with intricate hand carving and a silver horn, and called Blue, his favorite mount, a long-legged Arizona gelding with powder-colored body, black mane and tail. Blue loved Jerry and would come when Addison appeared. Saddling up, Jerry joined

K.O. Pierce and the others of the crew, and they started south, hoping in the daylight to pick up the rustler sign.

Reaching the point where the attack had been made, a few miles south of the ranch-house, they cast about for tracks.

"Don't look so good," grumbled Pierce. "That cussed storm washed out the all-fired cussed tracks, fellers."

CHAPTER II
KO OUTFIT

With no trail to follow, they drifted south, but late in the afternoon they had come on nothing to help them in the search. The country was wild, broken by sharp-toothed ridges, by deep gashes in the red earth. Thick, thorned brush and tortuous cactus growths barred the way. It was said that every plant in the Big Bend either "sticks or stings," and Addison was ready to agree.

Mountain lions prowled the thickets. They were always hungry and ready to spring on a calf that strayed from its long-horned parents.

The men were willing to quit the chase as the sun threatened to redden over the western hills. They had reached a spot where a plume of smoke showed in the south.

"What's that, I wonder?" asked Addison. He was making his first trip to the Big Bend country.

"That comes from Mariscal," replied Pierce. "Little Mexican settlement down there."

"Yeah," growled Rob Henderson, a lean, tobacco-chewing rider, "and I'll bet them Mexicans could tell yuh where Chihuahua Pete hides out!"

"Only they wouldn't," said another cowboy.

Cursing everybody in general and Mexican rustlers in particular, they turned and rode back toward the ranch, the fruitless search ended.

During the run, Addison had sighted several small bands of horses. Through the field-glasses, he had been able to see that some carried the KO brand, and Pierce confirmed it. But once they had drifted into the mountains they were hard to find.

The next morning, Addison told Pierce he was going to run down to see about building a trap into which the mustangs they had seen might be driven. They were worth money, and Pierce was enthusiastic over Addison's plan.

Addison took Blue, his own horse, and provisions. He rode slowly through the hills, and came quite close to a number of the wild horses. Before long he found a narrowing way into which they might be driven, where a hidden pen would contain them.

He camped out that night, and continued his survey the next day. His travels brought him quite close to Mariscal, which the KO men had said was the name of the Mexican village from which the smoke had come.

He came out on a rutted dirt road, over which carts might be driven, and Blue trotted south. After a time Addison reached a point from which he could see the little settlement.

It was built on the creek bank, and there were only fifteen or twenty structures, of adobe, with thatched roofs. A fence made of thorned bush enclosed the whole village. In the center was a low-roofed *hacienda,* larger than the other buildings. Addison could see Mexican figures in the dirt roads, and children and animals were playing about the homes.

As he stared at the place, a slight sound to his left caused him to turn. It was dangerous country, and a rider must always be alert.

But Addison froze in his saddle, as he saw that the slight sound had been made by a girl on a white mare. She was of Mexican blood, with blue-black hair, long-lashed dark eyes, and an exquisite, small body. Her beauty struck Jerry Addison hard, the

19

contrast of seeing a lovely girl in such a setting accentuating his emotion. Her eyes were startled as her gaze met his.

"*Buenos dias,* senorita," Addison greeted, finding his tongue.

But instead of answering she whipped her horse around, and flashed away. She was quickly out of sight in the brush.

Addison started to follow her, but after traveling for several hundred yards on the winding trail through the chaparral, ever nearer to the settlement, he decided that discretion was the better part of valor. He had evidently frightened the girl, and she had run from him. Quick-tempered, volatile Latin natures of her kin and friends might conclude he was a menace. From what Pierce and his men had said, there was bad blood between the Mexicans and the Anglo-Saxon elements here abouts.

Next morning, close to the noon hour, Addison rode up to the KO. He unsaddled Blue, cared for his horse, and turned the gelding out in the pasture. Washing up, he was ready for the hot meal which the cook was making ready.

His mind was on the pretty senorita he had glimpsed. He would recall that she was very lovely, but memory had its tantalizing way of refusing to retain definite features.

The encounter had made a deep impression on him.

"I'd like to meet her and talk to her," he kept thinking.

There were visitors at the ranch. Several horses stood with reins down in front of the main house. Addison rolled a quirly and strolled around. Pierce was sitting on the veranda with his guests.

"Hullo, Jerry," sang out Pierce, in his bull voice. "Have any luck?"

"Yeah, I seen a lot of hosses, K.O.," replied Addison. "And there's a good place for us to build a trap."

"Come on up and take the load off yore feet," said K.O. "Meet the folks, Jerry."

Pierce made the introductions.

"This here is Colonel Bart Farney," he said, with a wave of his hand to a tall lean man of military bearing. The hand moved to indicate the other man who was lanky and grinning. "And meet Turk Monroe, the Colonel's top man," said Pierce.

The Colonel cleared his throat, greeting Addison.

"Hem-hem! How do you do, young man," the Colonel said, shaking hands. "You're a bronc buster, aren't you?"

Colonel Farney was a fine figure of a man,

and the tips of his brown mustache, which were waxed and turned up, twitched when he smiled. His teeth were even and white, his brown hair was parted in the middle and plastered to his round head, and the pink flesh of his cheeks was shining, from much scrubbing. His clothing — a dark-brown jacket, fawn-colored riding breeches, and shining black boots — was spotless. But even as young Addison shook hands, his eyes were on the metal flower in Colonel Farney's buttonhole. It was perhaps an inch in diameter, and crimson in hue, with a yellow center.

"Turk" Monroe, Farney's aide, grinned at Addison as they shook hands. Lanky Monroe had a long turkey neck from which his Adam's-apple protruded. As he smiled — on one side of his mouth — yellow buck teeth showed. He wore leather pants and a buckskin shirt, and had pushed back his Stetson. He, too, wore a crimson metal flower.

There were two other men in riding clothes whom Pierce introduced, but Farney and Monroe stood out in the group.

"As I was sayin' when yore bronc buster so rudely busted in," said Turk Monroe, winking at Addison, "this here feller was talkin' on temp'rance, and says to the folks,

'S'posin' I had a pail of water and a pail of red-eye on this here stage, and I brung out a donkey. What pail *you* figger he'd drink from?' And a cowboy jumps up and yells, 'He'd take the water because he's a jackass!' "

Turk laughed uproariously, and Pierce and Addison joined in.

But the talk was chiefly serious. Colonel Farney and Pierce were conferring on some matter of importance.

"I tell you, Pierce," Farney picked up what he had been discussing, "you ranchers must organize against these cow thieves! I heard of the terrible trouble you had and that's why I'm here. I'm organizing you cowmen into a protective society — the Crimson Flower." Farney touched the red badge in his lapel. "It's perfectly outrageous that such killers should be at large. But if we band together, our forces can handle anything the rustlers can bring to bear. We'll go after 'em, too, hammer and tongs. Turk here is an expert man-hunter. He's had a good deal of experience as a law officer. In fact, if you come in, we'll guarantee that the rustlers will never again touch your stock or harm your men."

"How yuh figger on lettin' the rustlers savvy about this Crimson Flower business?"

asked Pierce.

"We'll post the range, warning them off. Soon they won't dare strike any of our members. You'll see! Turk and his boys will chase 'em to Hades and back. After all, you haven't time to run for days huntin' the thieves, trackin' them down, as we would have. Besides, you know it takes experts to catch many outlaws."

"Well, it sounds good to me." Pierce nodded thoughtfully. "I reckon I'll join up. You say Charlie Matson done signed up?"

"Yes, Matson's with us. He lost a cowpuncher and a number of his cows to the same gang — Chihuahua Pete's bunch. Matson is wearin' the crimson flower now."

"Come and get it!" the cook's voice bawled. They all filed to the table for the noon meal.

Addison was busy during the next few days with his work. He thought of the pretty senorita he had seen, wondering who she was. He could not shake off the spell of her lovely eyes.

K. O. Pierce had joined Colonel Bartholomew's Crimson Flower, the protective association against Chihuahua Pete and others of his kind who preyed on decent men. Others, too, in the Big Bend, had signed up with Farney, and had paid their dues, in the attempt to see if they could keep their riders and herds safe.

Whenever Addison was riding out from the ranch, he soon noted new signs on posts — wooden plaques with words in red letters, warning off thieves:

```
NOTICE: THIS RANCH AND BRAND, KO,
ARE PROTECTED BY THE CRIMSON FLOWER.
RUSTLERS TAKE WARNING!
```

A metal flower was tacked on as signature, and below the English version was a Spanish translation.

One afternoon, a rider brought in news that George Young, a rancher whose home lay some miles east of the KO, had lost a cowboy and two hundred steers the night before, to Chihuahua Pete and his gang.

"Shucks!" growled Pierce. "Young wouldn't join up with us. But mebbe he'll change his mind now!"

CHAPTER III
BANDITS FOR
BREAKFAST

Sometimes the chronically startled clerk at Rangers Headquarters, Austin, Texas, fervently prayed that a barometer could be installed outside the office of Captain William McDowell. Then, the clerk believed, he might be able to judge the state of the good captain's temper, and advance or retreat to the cyclone cellar accordingly.

Bill McDowell, in charge of law enforcement for a huge chunk of the Union's largest state, and with no more than a handful of Rangers to do the job, was too old to ride the rough danger trails any longer. He could not, as of yore, gnash his teeth, curse, and leap into saddle, spurring to the theater of operations and settling the trouble then and there.

Nowadays as reports reached his desk, he had to use some other method, even though his naturally warm temper began to stew, then steam, like a geyser making ready to spout. This usually heated the atmosphere until suddenly the storm broke with all the violence of a squall at sea. Then all objects, animate or inanimate — sometimes Mc-Dowell accused the clerk of belonging to the latter category, along with stones, molasses and lead — were apt to be disturbed by the explosion.

The explosion had just occurred. The ink-well jumped two inches off the desk as Mc-Dowell's fist hit the blotter. He seized the bell and hurled it against the wall instead of ringing it in a normal manner.

His chair tipped over as he abruptly leaped to his booted feet and began pacing up and down, a caged lion. A twinge of pain from his stiff back sent a spasm across his wrinkled face, but he tried to ignore it as his thick, hoary eyebrows joined in a single, menacing line over his flaming eyes.

The clerk did not immediately pop into view at the hall doorway and McDowell started that way, fists clenched. But as the Captain heard a soft tread in the corridor, he stopped short, and waited. He knew those footsteps. Soon a tall man appeared, and grinned at the apoplectic Captain.

" 'Mornin', Cap'n McDowell," he drawled. "Clerk said yuh wanted me."

"That's right, Hatfield, I do want you, and

bad," barked McDowell. "But how'd that cuss savvy? He didn't come when I rung for him. He's got to get the lead out of his soul and step lively. He's slow as molasses. Might as well have a rock sittin' out there on that stool, workin' on them ledgers."

McDowell continued to grumble, but the presence of the tall officer soothed him.

In the outer offices, the clerk, who had correctly anticipated what the Captain's order would be, and had short-circuited the matter by immediately calling in Jim Hatfield, had picked up his pen again and was trying to finish a requisition list for a Ranger troop in East Texas.

36 cans bullybeef
6 cases hardtack
12 cussed bandits

With a cluck of dismay, the clerk realized that while listening to the agonized words which had been coming from McDowell's office, in his preoccupation he had written some of them down rather than the innocent ones called for in the requisition. With a violent expression directly stolen from McDowell's pet vocabulary, the clerk ripped up the sheet and started a fresh one.

From the office came the soothing mur-

mur of two gentlemen talking.

"Bad situation buildin' up in the Big Bend country, Hatfield," McDowell was saying. "I want some bandits for breakfast, savvy?"

"Yes suh."

Hatfield's voice was surprisingly soft, for such a big fellow. He topped six feet with his powerful body, broad at the shoulders, tapering to the narrow waist of the true fighting man. Here depended his two Colt .45 revolvers.

Bronzed by wind and sun and rain, in the pink of condition through his hard life spent in the open, Ranger Jim Hatfield had the strength of a fighting tiger. His heart beat with a flaming courage that never quailed before any odds. In repose, his gray-green eyes were almost lazy, yet they could darken in anger, flash with battle light. Then it was well for men to walk and talk softly.

He wore range clothing — thick trousers to ward off thorns and brush in riding, a clean blue shirt, and half-boots with silver spurs. Under his wide Stetson showed jet-black hair, that glinted as a sign of his health.

McDowell knew Jim Hatfield's speed and ability with guns. He knew the tall Ranger's muscular might and staying powers. But he also knew that to match these physical attributes, Hatfield had a diplomat's brain, a shrewd, analytical mind. Sometimes such faculties were more important than brute force.

Hatfield listened carefully to what his superior officer had to say. He knew that McDowell had all sources of information about Texas, that to the Rangers came the complaints of decent citizens, those who rightfully demand the State's protection. And the Ranger also was well-acquainted with McDowell's genius at sizing up a situation from afar.

"There've been sev'ral killin's down there, of cowmen and their boys," continued McDowell. He had a map of the Big Bend on the desk before him, and his gnarled finger indicated the section involved. "This here settlement is the town of Big Bend. It's not much more'n a widenin' in the road, but serves the scattered ranches in the district, savvy?

"Here, above the Chisos Mountains, lies the ranch country. K. O. Pierce of the KO brand has his home here, and runs his cattle on the open range. Charlie Matson, Square M, is another. Then there's George Young, of the Bar Y, and more. Word's come through to me that Pierce's brother and one of his cowboys were killed by rustlers and outlaws. Matson and Young have been shot out of the saddle, too.

"My information is that a Mexican bandit called Chihuahua Pete is operatin' in the district, stealin' cows and shootin' those who get in his way. I ain't got any prior information on Chihuahua Pete. Reckon he's come up from Mexico, prob'ly on the run from the Rurales, and they'd thank you if you sent 'em his hide, cured and branded."

McDowell paused, and Hatfield slowly raised his gray-green eyes to meet the steady gaze of the old Ranger captain.

"What else, Cap'n?" he asked.

"There is somethin' else. It ain't definite, though, like the outlaws. I hear that K. O. Pierce, and others in the Big Bend, have organized or joined a protective society called the Crimson Flower. They're after Chihuahua Pete and his gang and mean to wipe the rustlers out. Well, yuh can't blame men for bandin' together to save their hides. On the other hand, the Rangers should be able to maintain law and order so's such private troops won't be necessary. Yuh can check it up when yuh get down there."

There was a long pause, and Hatfield rose. He had noted what McDowell had told him, had picked out the route he would follow to the infected area, and had tabulated the names. His commission was indefinite, so he must be able to judge the matter when he arrived, and take the proper steps.

"One thing more," said McDowell, his voice softening. "South of the range I've spoke of is a small village named Mariscal. The folks are of Spanish-Mexican blood. But they're Texans, Americans that is, just as good as you or me. Yuh savvy that."

"I savvy."

"There's hot talk agin these folks, by the cowmen, Pierce included," complained McDowell. "They seem to suspect those folks of harborin' the rustlers. If they are, then they must be punished. But if not, yuh'll have to settle what looks like a war between the two factions."

It was a delicate point. To run down a dangerous bandit was comparatively simple, when placed alongside such a problem.

Armed with all the information McDowell's office could offer, and with the power of the State, Jim Hatfield shook hands with the old Ranger Captain and strode out into the brilliant sunshine.

McDowell watched from a side window, as the tall man saddled up a golden sorrel. Goldy, the beautiful gelding, was Hatfield's war horse, his companion of the danger trails. Swift and strong of limb, with a fighting heart, Goldy carried Hatfield on his missions to the far reaches of Texas.

Carbine in its boot, under one long leg, his Colts in their oiled, supple holsters, provisions and extra gear stowed in his saddlebags, Hatfield turned the golden sorrel southwest from Austin. He swung around once, and waved to the old man in the office window.

"I hope he comes back," muttered McDowell. "I'd rather lose myself than Jim Hatfield. . . ."

Hatfield had made a swift run of it from Austin, but he was still a hundred miles from his destination, Big Bend, the small settlement above K. O. Pierce's ranch, when he reached another small town not long before nightfall. Behind Goldy and the Ranger lay the Pecos, that alkaline river which, after its long, tortuous trip through deep-scored, mysterious canyons, joined the Rio Grande eastward of the Big Bend.

The Ranger had paused at the town to rest Goldy and refresh himself and the horse. He left the gelding at the livery stable corral, after grooming and seeing to the needs of the animal that was his closest friend and companion.

It was late afternoon, and the sun was reddening over the vast reaches of the Big Bend country.

"Yuh could lose half a dozen eastern states in her," mused the tall Ranger, his spurs tinkling as he moved along the wooden sidewalk, under the awnings built out from above.

The town was of fair size, serving ranching country to the north and west. It was on the railroad — a flag stop — and there were loading chutes and pens down the track from the little station. The main road ran north from the tracks and widened into a plaza, on both sides of which stood stores, saloons and houses. Several side streets branched off, petering out into the brush-covered wilderness.

Intent on getting a cool drink, and after it some warm, sustaining food to fill an aching void, the tall Ranger headed for the largest saloon. A sign outside, carrying a flamboyant picture of a great-horned steer, proclaimed the place to be the Longhorn.

There were citizens about, mostly keeping to the shade still, for it had been a hot afternoon. Some were townsmen, others cowboys. In front of the Longhorn stood a large collection of saddled horses, their reins thrown over the continuous hitch-rack which prevented animals at the curb from coming onto the sidewalk.

Riders were still coming into town, dismounting, and dropping their reins, then entering the big saloon.

Hatfield's Ranger star was carried in a hidden pocket, for he did not like to announce his presence by a badge. Always he preferred to work quietly until he had all the information he could gain. So there was no outward mark to proclaim he was a lawman. Judging by his clothing he might have been a waddy in town for a spree.

The new arrivals made a practice of ducking under the hitch-rack, to reach the porch of the saloon. One of them, straightening up, bumped into the Ranger.

He looked irritated for a moment, but seeing the size of the man he had jostled, he said pleasantly:

"Sorry, Mac. Didn't see yuh."

"Don't mention it, mister," replied Hatfield politely.

Suddenly the Ranger realized that the fellow who had run into him wore a metal crimson flower with a yellow center, attached to his shirt-pocket buttonhole. It was about an inch in diameter and easy to see.

And as he drew back, allowing the other men to pass, he noted that these all sported a similar decoration. They went into the

Longhorn, and through a window Hatfield could see that they all crowded up to the long bar.

"They're a long way from where I figgered they'd be," mused the Ranger. "Wonder if they're chasin' rustlers over thisaway?"

McDowell had mentioned the Crimson Flower organization. The men wearing the badge, the Ranger had noted all wore the usual range riding dress of leather chaps or trousers against thorns of the region, shirt and bandanna, and the sort of Stetson each happened to fancy.

They were armed, with carbine, or shotgun, and Colt revolvers. But so was every other rider seen on the open range. Some had dirt-stained or bearded faces, some were fat, some lean, short, or tall. The Ranger had seen range crews, cowboys and such, who looked no better or worse.

Thoughtfully, Hatfield trailed inside the saloon. The bar was crowded with thirsty customers. There were tables set about, and at these sat other drinkers. Some of them also wore the crimson flower.

One fellow attracted the Ranger's attention, as well as that of others. He was a tall, lean man, with a military bearing, and a brown mustache with waxed tips. His clothing was clean and of good material, and he had removed his hat to cool his head, showing brown hair plastered on a round head. The flesh of his face was pink from scrubbing. He wore one of the red flowers, and he was talking animatedly with a stout man of rancher type who, fingering his glass of red-eye, was listening attentively to the tall man's words.

The stout cowman wore no metal flower badge, but the bony man with a long turkey neck and prominent Adam's-apple who sat at the same table had a crimson flower attached to his shirt. He was smiling, a crooked smile that showed half of his yellow, horse teeth. His hat was pushed back on his head, and dust covered his leather pants and buckskin shirt.

Curiosity killed a cat, thought Hatfield, but it was a law officer's stock-in-trade. The Crimson Flower intrigued him, and he edged closer to the group at the table. There were forty to fifty others in the saloon who were wearing that badge, but they were lined at the bar or silently drinking at other tables.

Hatfield could catch a snatch of the tall handsome man's words as he drew nearer:

"I tell you, Williams," the fellow was saying, "you and other ranchers like you won't have any peace or safety unless you join us.

Chihuahua Pete's gang terrorized the whole range west of here, until we chased him out. He's moved over to another part of the country, and that's where your steers have gone. His gang shot down your cowboy."

"Mebbe you're right, Farney." The stout rancher called Williams nodded. The animated talker whom Hatfield took to be Farney had paused, and was taking a drink.

"Say, Williams," the man with the Adam's apple piped up, "ever hear of the dude they asked what cow-hide was used for? The dude says, 'To keep the cow together!' " The man laughed loudly at his own joke.

Farney frowned, as Williams grinned.

"All right, Turk," Farney said. "This is serious business we're talkin'. Never mind the jokes now."

"All right, boss." The man addressed as Turk subsided.

And it was at that moment that, from the corner of his eye, Hatfield saw someone down the bar turn quickly and hurry out the back way.

CHAPTER IV
RECRUIT

Keenly attuned, the Ranger sensed trouble. He was aware that the man had glanced his way just before he had hurriedly left the Longhorn.

"I'd better check up," he thought. "There was somethin' familiar about that feller."

It was always necessary for him to be wary of such encounters, for a chance recognition by some outlaw might spell ruin, even death.

Going out the front, Hatfield stepped over to look down the passage connecting Main Street and the back road. It was empty, and he moved toward the other side. He had luck there, for the fellow who had ducked from the saloon was coming hastily toward him. When he saw the Ranger's tall figure he stopped and, face to face, Hatfield knew who the man was.

"Howdy, Nemo!" he called. "Wait a jiffy!" His long legs took him swiftly to the man.

Nemo was a big man with dark hair. A Colt rode at his hip. But there was fear in his black eyes as he stared at Hatfield, and he licked his cracked lips.

"Hullo, Ranger," he muttered, and he swallowed hard. His fingers worked nervously.

"Ssh — not so loud, Nemo," said Hatfield. "I'm here on business."

A harsh rasp was in Hatfield's voice. His gray-green eyes were dark, his rugged jaw thrust out. Long fingers vised on Nemo's thick wrist.

Nemo, a minor member of an outlaw gang which Hatfield had smashed some time before in East Texas, had been sent to state's prison, and had served his sentence. And now here, across the Pecos, Nemo was wearing the Crimson Flower!

Hatfield thought fast. The fact that Nemo was a member of Farney's organization did not mean that the Crimson Flower was an outlaw band. It might be that Nemo had lied to those who had hired him, or he might even have reformed after finishing his prison term. On the other hand, such a person as Nemo might give away Hatfield's identity as a Texas Ranger. If it should be that the organization, or some individual did not want to be interfered with, an ambush could be laid before the officer was ready to mix it.

"I — I ain't done anything," growled Nemo.

"Who said you had?" asked Hatfield. "But I want to talk to you. Turn around and walk to the alley. I'll be at yore heels."

There were windows giving into the bar along the wall, and at any moment some of Nemo's companions might appear. Hatfield knew that — and so did Nemo.

For a moment he hesitated. He seemed about to resist, and Hatfield made ready to lay him out. However, Nemo apparently changed his mind. He walked toward the alley with a stiff-legged gait, careful to keep his arms out from his sides so that the Ranger might not misconstrue any motions he made with his hands. The back of his seamed, bulldog neck had turned dark-red.

This former rustler, whether reformed or not, had seen Jim Hatfield in action, had watched the Ranger shoot down several of the old gang who had dared resist the Texas Rangers. It had ruined Nemo's swashbuckling style. He now feared the Rangers' might above everything. He feared this one in particular.

"Which way?" mumbled Nemo, looking gingerly back over his shoulder.

"Turn right. See that stable? We'll go behind it."

Nemo obeyed, and Hatfield came up to him, facing the outlaw. Well aware of Nemo's thought processes, reading his alarm, Hatfield did not relax his tough, severe attitude. It served as a weapon in his work.

"What yuh want of me?" asked Nemo.

The cold, gray-green eyes of the Ranger drilled into Nemo's. The rustler looked down, his face muscles twitching.

"What're you up to down here, Nemo?" asked Hatfield.

"Who, me?" replied Nemo in a hurt tone. "Why, I come across the Pecos, figgerin' I'd get me a ridin' job where the Rangers wouldn't hound me."

"The Rangers never bother an hombre who's livin' right," Hatfield said grimly. "I asked what yuh're up to."

Nemo gulped. He looked quickly up at Hatfield, then his shifty eyes left the Ranger's.

"Yuh can't prove nothin'!" he mumbled. "I served my time, cuss it."

Hatfield's air was darkly menacing. He spoke in a slow drawl, accentuating each word.

"I ain't in the habit of takin' lip from such

as you, Nemo. Meetin' yuh has ruffled me, I'll admit. My finger itches. I don't feel safe with yuh around. Now, if yuh happened to be found dead, I reckon it wouldn't be no loss to anybody."

Scowling, the Ranger took a step closer, looming over Nemo. With what Nemo already knew about the officer, it was enough to break the rustler.

"All right — I'll tell you," he said hastily. "I joined up with the Crimson Flower riders day before yestiddy. Is that a crime?"

"I don't know yet," answered Hatfield. "I mean to find out. What'd they ask yuh when yuh applied?"

"Only could I ride and was I nervy enough to fire a hog-leg."

"I see," Hatfield laughed dryly. "Yuh come along, cold, and they hired yuh! Sounds likely."

Nemo gulped again. The silence grew thicker and thicker, as Hatfield eyed the ex-outlaw. At last Hatfield broke it.

"I reckon I'll run yuh out of town and tie yuh up somewheres, Nemo," he said, "till I can check up more on yuh. I aim to smear whatever goes on in the Big Bend. There've been killin's, which means that somebody's goin' to stretch hemp or swaller lead. I ain't leavin' these parts till it's all cleared up."

"How much do yuh savvy?" inquired Nemo curiously.

"More'n yuh think I do." The Ranger was grinning.

Nemo was obviously weighing the chances. Should he try to buck the Ranger, or should he give it all up as a bad job? He had no desire to be left trussed in the chaparral somewhere, until Hatfield could deal with him, and making a stab at shooting it out with Jim Hatfield was out of the question for him. He would not play against sure death.

"All right," he suddenly gave in. "I'll tell yuh all I savvy, Ranger."

"Don't call me Ranger agin, Nemo," ordered Hatfield.

"All right. I'll try to remember, R . . . What'll it be?"

"Make it Howes, Jim Howes."

"Howes," repeated Nemo. "Well, they done turned me loose from the pen in May. I fooled around the old town a while but it wasn't the same, so I lit out for the Pecos. One of the boys told me, before I left the pen, to look up a feller named Turk Monroe, who was needin' riders. I run into him, this Monroe, not far from here couple of days ago, and he said he'd give me a chance. We come here this afternoon."

"Why?"

"How should I savvy? Turk don't tell me or any of us riders why and wherefore. We obey orders. So far nothin' much has happened."

"This Turk Monroe's here now, ain't he?" asked Hatfield. "I heard that fancy gent with the waxed mustache call one of the fellers 'Turk.' Is that him?"

"That's Turk. The feller with the mustache is Colonel Farney, the big he-wolf, but I ain't seen him much."

"Farney appears to be Monroe's boss. That right?"

Nemo nodded. Mentally, he had slipped the noose, casting off his new associates. He was decidedly uneasy, for now he had not only Hatfield to fear, but the wrath of his new friends if they discovered he had double-crossed them.

Hatfield was turning it all over in his mind. He needed proof that Turk Monroe might be hiring rustlers, and men with prison sentences behind them to ride for the Crimson Flower. But he knew that on the range, nobody asked about a man's past, so long as he behaved himself.

"Who's the hombre back in the pen who sent yuh to Turk, Nemo?" demanded the Ranger.

Nemo hesitated again, but finally shrugged. He had told so much that more wouldn't make any difference to him, and anyway it was himself he was worrying about.

"George Kinny," he said. "He's doin' fifteen years for highway robbery."

"I've heard of Kinny." Hatfield nodded. "The Rangers caught him in Del Rio. . . . Well, come on, Nemo. Yuh're goin' to make me acquainted with Turk Monroe."

"Huh?" bleated the startled Nemo. "No, I ain't!"

The long fingers gripped Nemo's wrist.

"Yuh'll say you and me was cellmates together, that once we worked at the same game! George Kinny told yuh I was all right, savvy? And don't forget my handle — Jim Howes."

"Oh, what the . . . all right."

Nemo walked back toward the Longhorn.

"If anything goes sour, Nemo," said Hatfield softly, "you'll be first to catch lead."

A few minutes later, Hatfield slouched against the wall in the rear of the big saloon, while Nemo walked up to speak with Turk Monroe. The lanky man glanced at the tall man by the wall, as Nemo spoke with him, and then Monroe said something to Farney. The gangling Turk nodded and followed

46

Nemo, who came over to Hatfield.

"This here is Jim Howes, an old pard of mine," explained Nemo. "Kinny'll tell yuh he's all right, too. Jim here and me spent a year together in the same pen."

Turk smiled, one side of his leathery mouth opening, disclosing his yellow back teeth. His blue eyes were keen, as they sized up Hatfield.

"Shrimp, ain't yuh?" he said jokingly. When he spoke, his Adam's-apple jumped up and down. The turkey neck told where his nickname had originated. "Step in the back room and we'll have a pow-wow."

Nemo trailed after them. Turk Monroe led the way to a vacant room where they could talk without interruption.

"You want a job?" Turk said as he sat down. "Can yuh handle a Colt? Can yuh ride? The Crimson Flower — that's our bunch, see? — has man's work to do."

"Nemo'll tell yuh I can ride and shoot," drawled Hatfield.

"That's right, Turk," vouched Nemo hastily. "None better!"

"Good. If yuh're a pard of Kinny's and Nemo's, yuh'll be all right. Mebbe I'll give yuh a try-out." Monroe nodded. "As to how good yuh can ride, did yuh hear the story about the tenderfoot who boasted how good he could stick on a bronc? Well, they brung out a mustang, and the dude sails off and lands on his head in the dust. 'Hey, that hoss bucks somethin' awful!' howled the tenderfoot. And a cowboy says, 'Shucks! That bronc only coughed!' "

Nemo gave a sickly grin, as Turk, smiling at his own wit, waited expectantly. Hatfield burst into laughter.

"Ha-ha! Say, that's a beaut! First time I ever heard it. I'll have to remember it, but I can't tell a joke good as you, Turk. Do yuh savvy any more?"

"Plenty, Jim. Come on, let's go in and I'll stand yuh a drink."

Monroe's attitude had melted. He looked upon the new recruit as a fellow wit, who appreciated real humor.

As they went into the bar, Turk pushing a way to the front, a couple of men were swearing in loud voices at the dice they had been rolling.

"Reminds me of another, Jim," said Turk. "This here Texas man was struck by lightnin', see, while he was cussin'. 'That was mighty queer, wasn't it?' somebody says, and the other feller, says, 'Well, it'd be a sight queerer if lightnin' was to strike a Texas man when he *wasn't* cussin!' "

Hatfield laughed again uproariously.

Members wearing the red metal badge turned to look at him as Monroe, slapping him jovially on the back, pushed the red-eye bottle to him.

"Pour for yoreself, Jim," he invited. "Yuh're all right."

The Ranger, a good judge of human nature, had found a quick way to ingratiate himself with Turk. Monroe considered himself a humorist of the first water, and Hatfield's laughter was music to his prominent red ears.

Nemo threw down his whisky in one gulp. He was fidgeting uneasily.

"What ails yuh, Nemo?" Monroe asked. "Yuh act like yuh had the dance!"

Nemo scratched himself. "I think I picked up some fleas off that hound dog I was pettin' at the livery stable, Turk. I can't keep still."

"Well, go out and hop on yore bronc," said Monroe. "If yuh ride fast enough, it'll scare the fleas off."

Nemo nodded, and went outside. He caught Hatfield's eye before he left, gulped, and licked his lips. When Nemo had left, Monroe said:

"Nemo's all right, huh? Good old George wouldn't send anybody who ain't. Yuh worked with Nemo, yuh say?"

"That's right, Turk. I savvy Kinny, though, better'n Nemo."

The man with the waxed mustache, Farney, turned and signaled to Monroe.

"Wait a jiffy," said Turk. "I'll be right back."

Colonel Farney spoke for a moment with Turk, then Farney went out with the stout rancher and another man with whom he had been talking. It was growing dark. Attendants were lighting the lamps in the bar, and in other buildings lights were flickering on. Monroe returned to Hatfield, his new-found crony.

"We're goin' to spend the night here, Howes," said Turk. "What d'yuh say we have a real spree? Let's buy some bottles of redeye and go back in one of them rooms."

"Suits me fine, Turk," agreed Jim Hatflield.

CHAPTER V
ON THE MARCH

Monroe bought liquor, and called a couple more of the fellows wearing the red flower — pards of his. One was a black-bearded plugugly of about forty, addicted to language that was repellent, a man who had red-rimmed eyes and was shifty and quick. The other was younger, an oafish lad with a moon face and adenoids. That was plain enough, for he never closed his thick-lipped mouth.

Turk introduced the recruit to "Blackie" and to "Moon," sobriquets the Ranger thought fitting. With their bottles, the quartet repaired to one of the private rooms back of the saloon. A Mexican boy brought food on order — steak and potatoes, beans, bread, and apple pie.

"Hear about the cowpuncher who ordered steak?" said Turk when the four had been served. "The waiter fetched it to him purty near raw. 'Take that back and have it cooked!' says the waddy. 'It is cooked,' says the waiter. 'Why,' says the cowboy, 'I've seen steers hurt worse'n that get well!' "

Blackie, Moon and Hatfield all laughed. Blackie competed with the Ranger as to who would laugh loudest and longest, and the Ranger suspected Blackie of playing the same game he was, to ingratiate himself with Monroe by laughing at the jokes.

"Say, Turk," begged Blackie, "tell the one about the poker game!"

"All right," Turk said happily. "Seems this tough gang was playin' poker for big stakes, savvy? Suddenly the dealer throws his cards on the table, and jerks his six-gun. 'Boys,' he shouts, 'this game is crooked! Sneaky ain't playin' the hand I dealt him!' "

They all laughed again. Hatfield's mouth muscles ached, from twisting them in false mirth. The bottle was passed, and the cheap whisky burned the Ranger's throat like liquid fire. Monroe drank twice as much as his companions and much faster. He poured down a water tumbler full each time without blinking, taking it as though the stuff were beer.

It took several of these oversized drinks to show any effect on Turk, who plainly was a heavy drinker. Then Monroe became mellower. He grinned and laughed harder at his own jokes.

The room grew thick with blue tobacco fumes from the cigars and cigarettes smoked by the four men, and reeked with alcoholic fumes.

"You goin' to enlist Howes, Turk?" Blackie asked, after a time.

"Shore am. He's all right." Turk clapped the Ranger on the back. "Here, I forgot." He reached in his pocket and brought out one of the red metal flowers. It had a clasp pin, and Turk fastened it to Hatfield's shirt. "Yuh're now a member of the Crimson Flower, Jim," he said. "You stick with me. Yuh'll get yore orders from me, savvy?"

"That suits me to a T," declared Hatfield.

" 'T' stands for Turk," punned Monroe.

The evening was not too pleasant a one for Hatfield, who as a rule drank only when he was thirsty. The Ranger had no appetite for red-eye. But this was business. He went as slow as possible, but even so, the rotgut began to affect him as midnight approached. The close atmosphere choked him, used as he was to the clean air of the range. Still he realized that he had to laugh at Turk's jokes, and did. Blackie told one or two, but Moon, a stupid, dull-minded young giant was content to leave the honors to his companions. The four in the private room were satisfied with their own company while in the main saloon the other Crimson Riders whooped it up. The talk was of girls, of horses, of parties and bygone experiences mutual to the other three but not to the Ranger. He did not pick up any vital information. It was nearly two A.M. before Turk, raising another full tumbler of whisky to his lips, suddenly fell off his chair onto the floor.

Moon was already slumped in his chair, snoring. Blackie, hardly able to keep his feet, muttered, "Let him sleep — me, too," and half fell to the mat.

Hatfield went to the window, threw it up. He also was sleepy, and lay down on the couch, his head by the opening, where he could breathe some fresh air. . . .

It was late the next morning before Turk Monroe roused. The Ranger had already been out, washed up, and eaten some ham, eggs and had his coffee. He saw Colonel Farney arrive in town, consult with the newly aroused Turk, then Farney rode away.

At once Monroe gave orders.

"We're pullin' out, boys," he said to his men. "Soon as yuh've eat, saddle up. Half an hour."

To Hatfield, the recruit, he said:

"That was some party, huh, Jim? Wow, what a head I got this mornin'! Get yore hoss, and be ready to ride with us."

The Ranger picked up Goldy, saw to his horse, and saddled up, joining Crimson Flower men in the plaza as they collected. Several nodded to him.

Moon and Blackie were on hand, but though Hatfield looked around for Nemo, he did not see him. The Ranger began to worry a little.

Turk came out, riding a slate-gray gelding, a fine horse with lots of mettle. Monroe was an expert rider — that was plain at a glance to Hatfield, from the way the man could handle the dancing mustang.

Turk looked over his men. Then he frowned, and signaled to Hatfield. The Ranger pushed the golden horse to Turk's side.

"Where's Nemo?" asked Turk.

"I been watchin' for him, Turk," said Hatfield. "I ain't seen him."

"Go see if yuh can hunt the fool up. We're late now."

Hatfield was wary, on guard. He hurried through the settlement, but nobody had seen Nemo. And the ex-con's horse was gone.

"He's run off, shore as it's hot below!" decided the Ranger.

Frightened by the Ranger's arrival, Nemo had taken his leave.

Returning to Monroe, Hatfield reported:

"Somebody at the stable thinks they seen him ride out last night with a Mexican gal."

"Well, cuss the fool's hide, he can catch up with us, then!" growled Turk, whose head ached. "I ain't goin' to wait for him any longer."

He raised his hand, took his place at the head of his riders, and led the way westward out of the settlement. Monroe knew where they were going, and it was in the direction that Hatfield wished to ride — toward Big Bend.

They rode through the day, over rolling, brushy rangeland, now and then sighting bunches of longhorn cattle. Here were the strange plants of the region, the leather-button peyote, the St. Nicholas plant, and one called "It Blinds the Goat," from which fine spines would fly off into the eyes of any animal grazing too close to it. There were all sorts of cactuses, prickly pear, bayonet, and other forms of spiny growth.

Far away in the southwest rose the mountains, blue in the golden sky.

They spent the night in the chaparral, beside a waterhole, and resumed the run the next day.

It was around noon when they came into the little town of Big Bend.

There was something that passed for a road, a two-wheeled track in the brownish-red clay. Houses made of adobe brick and a few hovels clustered about the general store and single saloon, and made up the settlement. The store sold everything — cowboy gear, ranch supplies, ammunition, guns, provisions, canned goods, needles and thread, salt pork, clothing.

"Well, here we are, boys," said Monroe as he drew rein. "See to yore hosses and then take a drink and rest up. Get some shut-eye. Yuh may need it."

Turk dismounted and went over to one of the small buildings. Colonel Farney was in there, and Monroe went inside. From what Jim Hatfield could gather, this town of Big Bend seemed to be headquarters for the Crimson Riders.

Blackie was always with Hatfield, as he always seemed to be, no matter which way the tall Ranger turned.

"Come in," Blackie ordered Hatfield. "Yuh can hang up yore saddle in the shed."

"Just as you say, Blackie," said Hatfield companionably.

He had a good idea that Blackie was watching him, perhaps detailed to do so by

Monroe. Still there was the chance that Blackie, who was himself plugging for advancement by flattering Turk, was growing jealous of the big recruit who had so quickly ingratiated himself with the field chief.

Twenty-five yards to the rear of the general store stood a long carriage shed, open on one side. There the men were hanging their saddles on pegs, throwing down blankets and ponchos. They could sleep in here, and be sheltered from the elements. The shed was of timber with a thatched roof, but had been set on thick adobe bricks.

Hatfield chose a vacant corner for himself and his rig.

"Next on the program's to wet our whistles," said Blackie and the suggestion was received with enthusiasm.

On the way to the saloon they passed the building into which Turk had gone. On the door was nailed a larger replica of the red flower, symbol of Farney's protective society.

The saloon had only two windows cut in its adobe walls; the floor was of dirt, the bar planks set on kegs, and the red-eye served in battered tin mugs. A Mexican ran it. He also served *tequila* for those who wished it.

Blackie stayed with Hatfield. Again the

Ranger wondered if Monroe had ordered that. Had Nemo, stampeded by the Ranger's arrival, left some sort of warning message for Monroe?

Yet if this was the case, why had they not seized him during the night bivouac, as they might have done? A search of his person would have revealed that silver star on silver circle, emblem of the Texas Rangers, which Hatfield carried in a small pocket inside his shirt.

Hatfield was feeling his way as he worked into the gang. But the possibility that they might be engaged in lawful practices grew more remote as he came to know these men. Most of the riders were tough, experienced with guns. There was a certain suspicious manner, a shiftiness of eye in each, as he grew familiar with them, that such an expert as the Ranger attributed to outlaws. And if Monroe's bunch was dishonest, he knew they would kill a spy caught riding with them, without compunction.

So the little star burned against Hatfield's chest. It was the only piece of evidence which he had on him, but it would be a damning one among outlaws, who hated the Rangers as much as they feared them.

A number of the men were in the *cantina* when Hatfield and Blackie entered the place. They drank, and talked. After a couple of mugs of burning liquor, Blackie said:

"I'll pitch yuh a game of hoss-shoes, Howes."

Blackie escorted him down the street. They paused, as Turk Monroe, seeing them coming, came to the open door of Farney's office.

"Hullo, boys," Turk said. "Say, Howes, step over here a minute, will yuh?"

Colonel Farney was looking over Turk's bony shoulder, as Hatfield approached. The Ranger was aware of shrewd eyes that appraised his tall, powerful figure, and fixed his gaze.

"Lookin' me over," thought Hatfield.

"Hem-hem!" Farney cleared his throat. His waxed mustache twitched, and the bright light shone on his scrubbed cheeks. Hatfield himself needed a shave. He had purposely allowed himself to stay dirty, careless in appearance, so as to fit in with the majority of Turk Monroe's men.

Farney said nothing to Hatfield, but turned away after the mute examination.

"All right, boys, see you later," said Turk.

Blackie led the Ranger on, and Hatfield wondered if Blackie had brought him past the office so that Colonel Farney could have a look at the recruit.

In the side yard, by the store, spikes had been driven into the dirt and four horse-shoes provided an amusing game. Blackie and Hatfield enjoyed themselves until it was time to go back to eat.

The Mexican at the *cantina* cooked food, serving it in big iron kettles outside the kitchen door. There were greasy tin plates and the men dipped in for themselves. Most of them were accustomed to this, for they knew Farney had an arrangement with the saloonkeeper to furnish their meals.

That night, when they were all ready to turn in, Hatfield retired to his corner. He spread his blanket under him, and used his saddle for a pillow in the shed. It was too warm for him to need any cover.

Men about him were talking, jesting profanely, roughly, as was their wont. It was shadowy in the shed, although lights were still showing in Farney's quarters and in the saloon. Horses stamped the earth in the cor-rals. As the men finally quieted down, snores began to reverberate in the place.

Hatfield had nerves of steel. He could sleep on a hair-trigger. He dozed off.

Suddenly he started awake, hackles up, Colt gripped in his hand. There was some-one close by him, at his saddle-bags.

Hatfield lay quiet, his long lashes shading his eyes. He saw a man squatted within a yard of his head, stealthily examining by touch and the moonlight shafting into the open front of the shed, the objects in the Ranger's bags. The light was dim, but by the figure Hatfield thought it might be Blackie.

The prowler, who worked with the soundless skill of an expert thief, turned, and stared down at the prostrate Ranger, who feigned to be asleep. Hatfield could see the dark beard on the man's face. He was sure that it was Blackie.

"Checkin' up," he decided, for he could see that Blackie had taken nothing from the bags which had been hung on a peg.

Blackie had turned in near him. More heavy snores in the shed covered what slight noises he made in moving about.

Blackie waited for a minute or two, though it seemed much longer to the expectant Ranger. Hatfield's gun lay along his thigh. His hand was on it, but that was not unusual, for most men of the sort he was supposed to be slept with a Colt handy.

CHAPTER VI
DANGER

Blackie slowly came to Hatfield's side. He squatted down, and the Ranger could hear the man's breathing.

Blackie reached out a hand to feel, lightly, of the supposedly sleeping recruit's pockets. The searching fingers drew too close for safety to the Ranger star inside Hatfield's shirt, and the officer grunted, as though in sleep, and shifted his position. Blackie, not to be discouraged, waited until he quieted, then tried again.

It would be fatal to Hatfield's plans to have Blackie feel the shape of the badge. Something must be done.

"Ugh!-ugh! What the devil?" Hatfield pretended to awaken abruptly.

"It's all right, Howes," Blackie said hastily. "I'm out of tobac, that's all, and I didn't want to wake you. I ain't been able to sleep and I want to smoke."

"Huh! Here — plenty in this sack." Hatfield's voice was sleep-drenched.

From his breast pocket he took his bag of tobacco and handed it to Blackie, who drew off, and rolled a cigarette.

It was a close call. The Ranger had a faculty of sleeping lightly, and awakening at the slightest warning, but he realized that the silver star was a menace.

"I'll have to hide it and pick it up later," he decided.

Blackie was smoking, and Hatfield rolled over with his face to the wall. Close at hand was the adobe foundation on which the shed had been set. Rats and other gnawing rodents had burrowed under the bricks, and there were a number of such holes within easy reach. Carefully the Ranger worked his star out, and with his fingers pushed it into a crevice, under the foundation. The sandy dirt was loose, and he covered the badge with soil. . . .

An hour later, Blackie tried again. This time, the Ranger kept on snoring gently, and Blackie went over him, hunting for telltales. When he was satisfied, Blackie went back to his blankets. He had taken nothing from the recruit, and obviously it was a check-up. . . .

The next day was cloudy. A hot wind blew gritty dust through the disturbed air. Hatfield hung around town with the others. Some played cards or dice, while others drank, enjoying idleness.

The Ranger saw little of Turk Monroe, whose quarters were in the rear of Farney's office. Attempts to draw Blackie into boasting of the Riders and their exploits came to nothing. He, like the others, was close-mouthed when entirely sober.

That night, an hour or two after turning in at the carriage shed, the Ranger was roused by stirrings about him. Dark shadows loomed as men quietly rose, took their saddles, and went out. He watched a score of Riders go, and finally he sat up.

Immediately Blackie said:

"Go back to sleep, Howes. It's just some of the boys goin' out for a while."

"I'm wide awake, Blackie," said Hatfield. "Let's go along with 'em."

"Not tonight," said Blackie. "Maybe another time."

"Where's Turk?" Hatfield said complainingly. "I'll ask him can I go."

"Turk's busy. Yuh can talk to him when yuh see him." Blackie was snappish. "Go on back to sleep, I said."

To have pressed the issue would have aroused suspicion and done no good. Hatfield was forced to remain in the shed, as a body of horsemen pounded off from the settlement. When morning came there were only a dozen men around, among them Blackie.

Late in the afternoon, Turk Monroe led his riders back to Big Bend. They were dusty, weary, and hungry as wolves, and after eating, they turned in and slept.

"I'll have to push 'em," mused the Ranger, "if I want to get anywheres."

Around nine P.M., Moon, who had been out with Turk and his men, came into the saloon where Hatfield and his constant companion, Blackie, were playing a game of seven-up by the light of a smoky lantern.

"Hey, Pedro, let's have a bottle of *tequila* for Turk," sang out Moon.

Hatfield rose. "I'm goin' over and speak to Turk, Blackie. Reckon he's awake."

"Aw, let's finish the game," Blackie urged.

But Hatfield went out with Moon. Blackie followed him, and they went to the lighted office. Turk was sitting inside, his booted feet on the desk.

"Come in, boys," he said.

He had had a nap, after his ride, and was thirsty. Moon poured drinks in tin cups as Hatfield looked about the office. On the wall were maps of Texas and of the Big Bend district, with ranches in that section marked by their brands. There was a file, and a stack of papers stuck on a spike holder. The little office looked like the headquarters of a business house.

Colonel Farney was not around. As a matter of fact, Hatfield had not seen him for a couple of days.

After a few drinks, Turk softened up. Monroe told a joke or two, at which Hatfield and Blackie vied in laughing.

"Looka here, Turk," said Hatfield, seizing a moment. "I like you fellers mighty well. But Kinny told me I'd see some sport down here if I joined yuh. I'm sick of sittin' on my hunkers in this cemetery. If it's all the same to you, I'll mosey on in the mornin'."

Turk frowned, and shook his head.

"Don't say that, Howes," he said, and put an affectionate hand on Hatfield's shoulder. "Stick with me and we'll be runnin' the world before long. We're just testin' things out in these parts." He swept a bony hand toward the wall maps. "It's all figgered out. We aim to spread all over Texas."

"Well, spreadin' is what I crave," declared Hatfield. "I hate settin' still for long. I got another prospect near El Paso, so I'll pull out in the mornin'."

There was a silence. Moon and Blackie watched Turk Monroe for his reaction. Jokes or not, Turk was a tough customer. No man could boss such a gang as rode under him unless he was a killer and a strong character. There was a hard set to his crooked mouth and his eyes were dark as he said to the Ranger:

"No, you stick with us. I ain't goin' to turn yuh loose. Blackie says yuh're all right, and a pard of Kinny's is aces with me. Thing of it is, we have to be careful of new men. You savvy that some smart hombre might come along spyin'. In that case it would be kind of bad for him." Turk patted his six-shooter.

It was obvious that Turk, liking Hatfield, was being patient. But Hatfield feigned that he was wounded, his feelings hurt.

"Shucks!" he grumbled. "Yuh don't think I'm that kind of sidewinder, do yuh?"

" 'Course not," Turk said hastily. "If I did, yuh wouldn't be here settin' on yore high hoss like yuh are. I promise yuh this: I'm goin' over to the KO ranch tomorrer, and I'll take yuh with me. Next time there's anything really doin', we'll try yuh out. Now that's settled. Here, have a snifter. Did yuh hear the one about the gal named Helen Green . . . ?"

It was dinnertime when Hatfield rode up to the KO Ranch, following Turk, Moon, Blackie and a couple more of the Crimson

68

Riders. On the warm air came the appetizing odor of coffee, stew and hot biscuits cooking in the kitchen.

"Um, smells good," remarked Turk, as they left their horses in the shade after seeing to the animals. "Reckon we'll eat high today, boys."

Cowboys had come in from the range, and were heading toward the long shed, with board tables in it, which served as a dining room. As Hatfield trailed Turk and his bunch across the dusty yard toward the house, they crossed the path of a slim young man in leather chaps and a clean shirt. His freckled face was shaven, his deep-blue eyes had a steady, honest look as he regarded Monroe and the others with expressionless features.

His gait was stiff-legged. He limped slightly, but as he found he might come in front of them he paused; his back was straight, for he held himself well. Hatfield noted that under his "Nebraska" hat showed crisp, reddish hair.

"Howdy, Addison," sang out Turk.

"Hullo yoreself," the young man addressed as Addison replied coolly.

He waited for them to pass, and his quick glance touched the Ranger. There was a faint twist to his lips, as though he were looking at something he didn't much like when he regarded Monroe.

Turk Monroe turned to speak to him.

"Yuh changed yore mind about joinin' the Crimson Flower, Addison?" he asked. "All good men got to stick together. Lots of advantages in it for yuh, too, and cheap for a feller like yoreself. Only ten dollars per year dues, and we guarantee yuh protection against cow and hoss thieves."

"Obliged — but I can protect myself," said Addison. There was faint derision in his tone, though not enough for Monroe to pick it up and resent it.

"Yuh think so?" Turk said. "Well, some fellers figgered like you do, but later found they'd made a bad mistake."

Monroe shrugged, and moved on toward the front, while Addison continued toward the kitchen. When Addison was out of hearing, Turk growled:

"I don't cotton to that mealy-mouthed bronc buster! He thinks he's better'n we are. I'd like to take him down a peg, just for the sport of it."

"Well, why don't we?" said Moon.

"Who is he, exactly?" inquired Hatfield.

"Bronc buster by the name of Jerry Addison," explained Blackie. "He's workin' here for a while, gentlin' mustangs for Pierce."

At the front door, a large, bearded Texan with a red face and hair graying at the temples, greeted Monroe.

"Glad to see yuh, boys. Yuh're just in time for grub."

"Howdy, Pierce," Turk said, nodding. "Shore we'll stay for dinner. We was ridin' over thisaway and thought we'd drop in and see how things're goin'. Had any more rustler trouble?"

"No, I ain't," said the rancher. "But night 'fore last, Rob Rawson of the Diamond R lost some cows. It was Mexicans, they say — prob'ly Chihuahua Pete's gang again."

"Tough luck for Rawson," said Turk. "He wouldn't join up with us, though, so it ain't up to us. If yuh have any more fuss with them cow thieves, jist let us know, Pierce."

"I shore will," said the rancher.

The bell was ringing, and Pierce led them to the table in the rear shed, where he ate with his men. He was a widower, and his two daughters who had grown up and married were living elsewhere.

Hatfield kept quiet. He had heard about K.O. Pierce from McDowell when the Ranger captain was briefing him before his journey. Pierce had lost his brother and a cowboy to the outlaws, besides many cows. And there were other ranchers in this vicin-

71

ity who had suffered.

As yet, Hatfield was not sure how the Crimson Riders fitted into the picture. From what he had learned, however, he was growing surer and surer that they were a menace, not only to the Big Bend but to Texas. He intended to string along with Monroe until he could delve deeper into the secrets of the protective organization. After the narrow escape back in the carriage-shed, he had left his Ranger star buried under the foundation. So now to all outward appearance, he was a Crimson Rider.

Hatfield enjoyed the sustaining hot meal. They all sat on the front veranda after dinner, smoking, and the Ranger listened to the talk as K.O. Pierce and Turk Monroe discussed the price of beef, and other interesting subjects.

Jerry Addison rode over on a fine horse, a powder-colored gelding with black mane and tail. He had an expensive saddle on Blue, as he called his mount. Binoculars and a hunting rifle hung from his leather seat, and his saddle-bags bulged with the rations he carried.

"Say, Boss, I may not be back for a couple days," he said to Pierce. "I'm goin' to work on that west wing of the trap."

72

"All right, Jerry," Pierce told him. "See yuh when yuh get back. Want any help? I'm short-handed right now but I could spare a couple men, if you need 'em."

"That's all right," answered Addison quickly. "I'll handle it alone, Mr. Pierce. I got things well along."

He nodded, raised his hand to wave goodby and, turning Blue, trotted his horse away, turning south.

"How long yuh reckon Addison'll be around, K.O.?" inquired Turk.

"Oh, another month or two," said the rancher. "He's a smart lad. Best with hosses I ever see. He's been down there in the hills, studyin' them wild ones with his bring-'em nears, and he's buildin' a trap to drive 'em into. When he's ready, we'll all go down and help run 'em in. He say there's hundreds of mustangs in them mountains, and the money'll help make up for the beef I've lost to them cussed Mexican outlaws." Pierce frowned. "Turk, yuh ought to check up on them Mariscal *vaqueros.* Luis Contreras is boss in their village. I got a hunch they hide out Chihuahua Pete when he's on the run. Them folks stick together."

"Mebbe yuh're right," Turk said thoughtfully. "Yuh say Addison's camp is near the Mariscal trail?"

"I didn't say, but it is. Yuh savvy Elephant Knob? Well, Jerry has his camp on the trail side. The trap he's buildin' is west of that."

Pierce had to go out to direct some work his men were doing, so Turk Monroe took his leave. With Hatfield and his other riders, Turk rode away from the KO as though heading for Big Bend, but once over the rise, out of sight of the ranch and screened by a brush-topped ridge, he swung his horse south.

"Come on," he ordered. "We'll see about that bronc buster. I don't like him, and that hoss of his would fetch a thousand dollars anywheres."

Addison had an hour's start, but Turk was in no hurry. He knew about where the young man's camp lay and he did not want Addison to realize that he was being followed.

KO cows grazed in the grassy sections. Patches of brush and rock outcrops showed as the riders moved on south. The Ranger could identify many kinds of cactuses, and the peyote plant, as well as many other growths peculiar to the Big Bend. In the distance, the mountains appeared blue.

They stayed on the bronc buster's trail through the hot afternoon hours, careful not to get too close.

It was close to nightfall when, from a height, they saw their quarry ahead of them, still riding Blue southward.

"That's Elephant Knob, over there, but he ain't turned into it," grunted Monroe. "Stay back, boys. We don't want him to spot our dust."

Turk had a long-range rifle in a waterproof leather case, riding under his bony left leg. The Ranger believed that Monroe would drygulch the bronc buster with this fine weapon, from a safe distance, once Addison stopped moving and went into camp.

"I've got to keep 'em from killin' him," he told himself.

He hated to lose the advantage that he had gained, but he could not permit Turk to shoot a fine young man like the bronc buster. But he knew that when he did call the turn to save young Addison that it would be against odds of five to one. For besides Moon and Blackie in this party, there were two other Crimson Riders along — a silent member called "Jack" and a stout one everybody called "Fats."

Turk focused his field-glasses, his "bring-'em-nears" as he described them.

"Why the hombre's goin' right on!" he announced.

There was a wagon track coming in from

the northeast and when Jerry Addison reached the fork he kept riding south. The country was hilly and heavily bushed, with woods here and there, and Turk picked up distance. Then in the late afternoon sky, they saw smoke ahead.

"That's Mariscal, the Mexican village," said Blackie.

From a hilltop, they watched as Jerry Addison rode up to the gate of the walled settlement. It was surrounded by a high palisades made by weaving thorned brush and vines together on a framework of upright staves driven into the loose earth.

The gate was opened for Addison. The watching riders could see a high-peaked sombrero, and there were others about the little place.

"Dog my hide!" exclaimed Turk, and swore. "Come on! I'm goin' to find what he's up to, the cuss!"

As Turk swung down from the saddle, the other riders followed suit, including Hatfield. He realized that they were greatly surprised at Addison's visit to the Mexican village. It was apparently something they hadn't expected he might do.

Chapter VII
Treasure

Dark had plunged its mysterious curtain over the wild Big Bend. To the south lay the deep canyons of the Rio Grande. About the men who were following Turk Monroe's lead was the whispering wilderness.

In that tiny oasis that was the Mexican settlement, lights glowed yellow.

Fats had been left behind, to hold the horses and keep them quiet while the other men explored afoot. Turk, Hatfield, Moon, Blackie and Jack were now approaching the palisades surrounding the town of Mariscal.

"If them Mexicans catch us," whispered Blackie, "they'll carve our hearts out, Turk."

"They won't," answered Turk. "I got to know what that Addison hombre is doin' here. He done went into that *hacienda.* Come on — we'll see what he's up to. Blacken yore faces and hands so's yore skin won't shine."

Hatfield, with the others, rubbed dirt on

77

his face and hands, and was ready to go on in the dark.

The moon had not yet risen. A warm wind rustled the dry leaves of the bush, as the men crawled after Turk, up to the fence. There Turk Monroe began scooping out a hole with his long knife.

Hatfield and Moon dug in to help him. They made good progress for the soil was loose and sandy. After fifteen minutes of work, they were able to squeeze between the two uprights they had pushed aside.

There were lights in the nearby *hacienda* and in some of the shacks. Most of the inhabitants of the settlement were indoors, but there was a sentry at the main gate which was barred for the night.

Hatfield stayed close to Turk. The lanky man moved with Indian stealth, and showed a skill at the work which surprised the Ranger, who was himself expert at stalking. Monroe had real talents, a command over his fellowmen, and all the necessary attributes to be successful in the West, but his nature was as crooked as his mouth. A great waste, according to the lights of the tall Ranger.

Turk, with Hatfield creeping at his heels, got in under an open window at the back of the house. He rose up and peeked in, and

Hatfield, just behind him, could see over Turk's shoulder. The lighted interior was beautifully furnished, with fine chairs and divans, with hand-woven mats on the floor, and with a great refectory table standing on the opposite side. Candles in silver and golden candlesticks, and oil lamps gave off pleasant light.

But what caught the startled attention of both men was what was on the long table. It was a collection of rare objects seldom seen. Hand-beaten gold plates, urns, and drinking-mugs, holy objects such as crosses and strings of beads, gleamed in the soft light. Many of them were heavy, with a richness which told at once that they were of real precious metals. On the walls hung more *objets d'art,* and there were vases and pitchers, on sideboards, all over the large room. But the table was the center of the collection.

Hatfield could tell at a glance that the value of the stuff in that room would run into many thousands of dollars, and that some of the items would be found on examination to be priceless antiques. He was remembering that in the first centuries from America's discovery by the Spanish, that the Jesuits and other *padres* had come to this wilderness. The priests had converted many Indians and had taught them all sorts of crafts and skills, had supplied many new patterns and a religious incentive for the deft fingers of the native artisans. Gold, silver and copper had been used in making these lovely objects.

Hatfield heard Turk's gasp as the man's greedy eyes feasted on the glinting treasures. But his main attention was on that room.

There were people in the big room, and one of them was Jerry Addison. The bronc buster had taken off his Stetson and sat on a cushioned bench near a middle-aged Mexican gentleman who smiled as Addison talked to him in Spanish.

The don had a triangular spade beard, which accentuated the proud lines of his high-bred face. His eyes were dark, and his hair once had been, but now was whitening with his years. His suit was of soft maroon velvet, and a wide sky-blue sash was wound about his waist. Close at hand on a serving-table stood a bottle of wine, glasses, a plate of cakes.

In a straight-backed chair, hand-carved from some ebony wood, sat a lovely girl. Her small body, exquisitely formed, was set off by the silken gown she wore. In her raven hair was a jeweled comb. Her long-lashed eyes were cast downward, but now and then she would glance up and smile at Addison.

"I see why that mustanger's here!" thought the Ranger, a great light dawning. "Why, that little gal's as purty as an angel!"

An older woman, her hair smoothed back, sat primly beside the girl. She was crocheting, her nimble fingers flying at the work. She had a sweet face, and Hatfield thought she might be the girl's mother, or perhaps an aunt, acting as duenna. But after seeing the young senorita, Hatfield was convinced that young Addison was no fool. Such a beauty would draw the best of men — or the worst, for that matter.

The Ranger had to watch Turk for fear Monroe would jerk his Colt and kill Addison out of hand, for the bronc buster was an easy target in the lamplight.

"Now let us talk Eng-lash," Hatfield heard the young man's host suggest. "We hav' practise our Span-ish enough."

"All right, Senor Contreras," replied Addison. "In English or Spanish, what I got to say means the same. You want to be careful, mighty careful. That's why I come to see yuh the first time."

"Also," Hatfield added to himself, "because I'll bet yuh'd had a peek at that senorita!"

"*Si,* I have been worried." Contreras nodded. "I would no more allow Teresa to ride out far from the village."

"A good idea," Addison agreed. "I want to ask yuh agin, now that yuh savvy me better: Have you, or any folks in yore town here, ever helped or even seen this Mex *bandido,* Chihuahua Pete? It's important yuh tell me straight."

Contreras stopped smiling. He pursed his lips, shook his head.

"On my word, senor," he said, "we have nuzzing to do weeth Chihuahua Pete, or any other *bandido,* for zat matter."

"Yuh're shore none of the *vaqueros* here could savvy him, without you findin' out?" insisted the young bronc buster.

"As certain as of anytheeng. Seence you firs' ask me, I have inquire' close-ly. Why, none of us ever hear' of Chihuahua Pete till few weeks ago! He mus' have come from long way off, down een Mejico."

Addison stared at the don, whose gaze was straight and honest.

"I believe yuh, senor," he said at last, and nodded. "But K.O. Pierce and the other ranchers in the Big Bend think yuh help and mebbe hide them rustlers. It's a dangerous situation, Don Luis."

Contreras heartily agreed. "Ees why I tell my *amigos* here not to ride far from home, not to clash weeth Pierce's *vaqueros.* We are simple people, senor. We have our goats, our cattle, we raise our gardens, too. Now and zen, our *vaqueros* capture wild horses to sell. Zat's all."

"Well, you lie low and keep yore boys under control a while longer," advised Addison. "I may be able to work it all out. I found a secret camp in the mountains while I was huntin' mustangs in the monte. Here's somethin' I picked up near there."

Addison reached in his breast pocket and held something to the light. It was one of the metal flowers sported by Farney's Riders.

"I ain't said anything to Pierce yet," continued the mustanger, "but I'm watchin' that hidden camp regular, hopin' to see who's usin' it, savvy? 'Course, the Crimson Riders may have happened to drop one of their badges while huntin' Chihuahua Pete in the chaparral. But I got my own suspicions."

"Eef you need help, you mus' call on me," said Contreras. "I fur-nish *vaqueros* who are good fighters."

"I'll do that. Meanwhile, yuh got the makin's of a mighty bad factional war in these parts, between Pierce and his friends and yore own people. A wrong shot or two might start blood flowin' like water."

Turk Monroe shifted, and Hatfield was ready to throw himself on the man and keep him from shooting in at Addison. But Turk had changed his mind. He touched Hatfield, and began backing off, the others with him.

They had nearly reached the palings when a warning hiss from Turk sent them flat on the warm, sandy soil. A yellow mongrel, one of the village dogs, had come around Contreras' *hacienda,* and was approaching them. He had his muzzle down, perhaps tracking a rat or some other animal. They could hear him sniffing. He came nearer, and suddenly got their scent.

"Wuff!" The cur's hackles rose with his nose.

Turk reached for him, to throttle him, but the dog leaped back, snapping and began a furious barking that sounded as loud as the crack of doom.

No one who knew dogs could mistake the animal's message of alarm, and men came running from several of the shacks. There were servants of those who lived in the hacienda, and when they rushed out they were armed with shotguns and pistols.

"Run for it!" gasped Turk, cursing at the unlucky chance which had brought the dog upon them.

From a back door came a Mexican armed with a sawed-off shotgun. Seeing the dark figures of the intruders, he screamed a warning and threw up his weapon. Before the Ranger could stop Turk Monroe the man fired his Colt, the gun blasting fire in the darkness. The Mexican's hands flew up, the shotgun fell, and he on top of it.

Blackie was squeezing through the getaway hole, with Moon at his heels. Jack was already through. Hatfield and Turk were turned toward it, awaiting their chance to make it.

"Take this from the K.O.!" shouted Monroe in a stentorian voice which rang over the settlement. He emptied his pistol at the shadowy figures coming toward them.

The village was in a sweat of alarm. *Vaqueros* were shooting at shadows, yelling to one another.

Addison, Colt thrown up, and Don Luis Contreras with a fowling-piece in his hands, dashed into the fray. Monroe's blood lust had been aroused and, filled with fury, he raised his reloaded six-shooter, taking aim at Addison and the don.

With a quick lunge, Hatfield bumped against Turk, and the killer's shot went wild.

"What the devil!" snarled Turk.

"Come on, Turk, crawl through!" Hatfield urged. "They'll massacree us!"

The ruse worked. Monroe thought that Hatfield was in a hurry to escape, rather than that the big man wished to save lives. Discretion getting the best of him, Turk dived into the hole like a rabbit, his long legs squirming as he wormed his way through.

Bullets and buckshot hunted the Ranger, spattering the fence, kicking up the sand as he followed Turk. Hatfield was flattened out, but the defenders of the settlement were too close for comfort, and the singing lead gave him real impetus as he hunched his wide shoulders to get under the palisade.

When he came to his feet outside, Monroe was already running after Blackie, Moon and Jack, who were making for the horses. Behind them, the Mexican settlement howled.

Fats had the horses ready, and the men leaped aboard. They had gained time, for the pursuers would have to get their mustangs, go through the gate on the other side of the town, and come all the way around in the darkness before they could pursue. Monroe led them as they rode for the monte.

Hatfield was not certain that his trick of

bumping Turk at the critical moment that the man had been taking aim at Addison and Contreras had passed for what it seemed. Monroe was clever as well as dangerous. Perhaps when Turk had time to think it over, he might turn against the new member of the Crimson Riders.

The moon was lightening the horizon but they could ride in the dense shadows of the bush. The angry Mexicans who followed never sighted the half dozen Riders as they retreated, northward, Turk leading the way and apparently familiar with the ground.

When they had put a couple of miles between the settlement and themselves, Blackie called: "Say, Turk, hold up a jiffy."

Monroe had been riding at a furious pace. The Ranger had stayed at his horse's heels on Goldy, but Blackie, Moon, and the other two were strung out, with Fats two hundred yards in the rear. Turk slowed, and brought his horse to a walk. Blackie caught up.

"I'm plumb tuckered out, Turk," complained Blackie. "I done cut my arm on a sharp rock crawlin' through that hole, and it's bleedin' like a stuck pig. What say we head for the camp and take it easy here?"

"All right," growled Monroe. "Mebbe Addison'll come snoopin' round while we're there. We'll have to give it up, though, since he savvies where it is. Cuss him, I'll learn him to spy on the Riders! Wonder who the fool was who dropped that badge near the cave?"

Well to the north of the village, Turk took a narrow side trail which led them west. The moon was up, and in the silver sky they could see the enormous bulk of Elephant Knob. Near here, Jerry Addison was building his mustang trap.

Monroe showed no hesitation as he led them. Plainly he knew this country backward and forward. He turned past the eastern face of the Knob, entered a deep-cut arroyo, a dry stream bed. Whenever it rained that arroyo carried the run-off water from the hill, and its bottom was paved with close-packed pebbles, so that tracks did not show after the horsemen had passed.

For nearly a mile they followed the arroyo, before Turk urged his horse up a sand bank and dismounted. With the others following closely, he led his mustang up a steep slope, and to a side ledge that was screened by thick brush. Here, hidden from spying eyes, was a cave entrance. The horses could stand in a recess on the south side of Elephant Knob.

The men entered the cave, which widened out into a large chamber. They had a cache there, and Moon and Jack got out some food and a bottle of whisky which they shared, by the light of a candle guttering in a rock niche close at hand.

The Ranger looked curiously about. There were obvious signs that men had been here — candle drippings galore, the cache of boxes in which food was kept, and in the rear of the cavern he thought he saw clothing hanging from the walls. They had blankets, too, and a spring formed a pool not far away.

Blackie's wound was a painful one. It was a couple of inches long, and had been made by the sharp edge of a rock he had pushed against in his hurry to get away. They washed it, and roughly bandaged it.

Then, spreading blankets, they slept.

CHAPTER VIII
ATTACK

At dawn, Turk was up, shaking the other men. They arose and ate from the food cache. A little daylight filtered into the cavern, but the recesses were still black.

Monroe went to the opening and Hatfield trailed him. They could see for miles across the vast wilderness of the Big Bend. The Rio Grande, separating Mexico and the States, was lost in its series of deep canyons.

"You got to savvy yore way in these parts," remarked Turk. "I was born down thisaway and used to hunt through here with my old man." He turned and called to the others: "All right, fellers, let's saddle up. We got mighty important news to carry back to Big Bend."

"To Farney, I s'pose," thought the Ranger. If there had been any doubts in his mind as to the Crimson Riders being evil, they had certainly been thoroughly dispelled now.

While they were on the ledge, saddling

the horses, Blackie said:

"Hey, Turk, there's someone over on that west slope."

"Mebbe it's Lenihan," suggested Moon.

"Len ain't likely to come unless we signal him," growled Turk. "Wait'll I try my bring-'em-nears."

He reached his binoculars and began to focus them.

"Who's Lenihan, Turk?" Hatfield asked casually.

"Oh, he handles cattle for us now and then . . . Say, boys, that's Jerry Addison! The cuss is out early. Mebbe I can pick him off with my rifle."

Hatfield could see the figure of the rider on the hillside, moving slowly on a mustang trail. The sun was coming up, as Monroe lay on his stomach, and rested the long barrel of his fine rifle on the flat rock which Blackie moved into place.

There was little wind, and Turk knew his weapon. What made it worse for Jerry Addison's chances, the Ranger could not jog Monroe this time without betraying himself. It was a long range, but Turk was a good shot and he might well hit Addison in a vital spot.

The other men were all much interested in the attempt to drygulch the bronc buster and squatted just behind Monroe, staring at the horseman. Hatfield hastily and quietly unshipped his Winchester, wiped the barrel on his sleeve, and turned it to the sun, moving it in his hand.

Turk pulled trigger, but Addison had suddenly veered, and ridden behind some boulders out of sight.

"Missed, cuss it!" swore Turk. "He swung just as I squeezed!"

"Can I try for him with my Winchester, Turk?" asked Hatfield eagerly. "If he shows again?"

"No," growled Turk. "That's enough. Somethin' warned him."

Intent as all of them had been on watching young Addison, they had failed to note Hatfield's play, as he caught the sunlight on his metal rifle barrel. Such a flash would be visible for miles, though it might not be seen at the source. To any wildernesswise man such as Jerry Addison, it had been warning enough. So he had hastily taken cover when he had caught the scintillating stabs.

"Let's go over there and smoke him out, Turk," suggested Moon eagerly.

"It'd take all day," said Turk. "Anyways, he could pick us off one at a time from that kind of cover he took to. Besides, we got to head back with our news. Clean up, and we'll ride."

They scrubbed the dirt from their faces and hands, mounted after leading the mustangs to the arroyo, and rode for Big Bend.

It was dark when they pulled into town. There were lights on in Farney's office, and Turk went direct to the headquarters of the Crimson Riders, to report. Hatfield tried to follow, but Monroe ordered him to go with Blackie and the others.

"We'll be ridin' at dawn, I reckon, Howes," said Turk. "Get some shut-eye and be ready to go. Yuh're goin' to get a real chanct for excitement."

An hour later, a dozen of the Riders saddled up and rode away, southwest, from Big Bend. They were fresh and rested, men who had not been out with Monroe. But what their mission was, the Ranger could not discover.

Lieutenants roused Hatfield and the other Riders early, before sunup. In the cool of the new day they breakfasted, then Monroe checked them over, as they mounted and lined up.

"Badges on, boys," he ordered. "Make shore yuh got plenty of ammunition. We got a long run ahead. Every man'll carry field rations for three days."

When they were ready to move out, Colonel Bartholomew Farney appeared, on a handsome black gelding which had one white foreleg. He was an excellent horseman, and looked spick-and-span in his neat riding clothing and Stetson strapped to his round head. The pink cheeks shone, and his mustache had a military twirl, points waxed upward to perfection. Farney wore a new crimson flower in his coat lapel.

"Hem, hem." Farney cleared his throat. There was a slight frown of self-importance on his face as he cried, "Follow me, men!" and took the lead out of Big Bend.

They drove southwest for a time, and then hit the trail to Mariscal, the village where Don Luis Contreras had his home.

Pausing only for a bite at noon under a sweltering sun, they kept on. About three in the afternoon, Farney signaled Turk, who rode up beside his chief. Someone had just hailed them from a patch of woods skirting the trail.

Monroe rode ahead, with several alert Riders, among them Hatfield. The man who had stopped them was one of the men who had left Big Bend the night before, and Turk signaled Farney and the main party to come on. The dozen Riders who had started earlier were holding a hundred head of prime steers in a nearby grove.

"Bring 'em out and drive 'em on," ordered Farney.

As the horsemen hazed the cows into the trail, Hatfield could read the brand, the KO seared into the hide of each animal.

The men led by Colonel Farney kept going, on the road to Mariscal, past the Elephant Knob trail.

"Wish Addison would show up," Monroe said to Hatfield. "If I spot him I'm goin' to fill him so full of lead he'll bust a bronc's back when he climbs on!"

"He's got it comin' to him," growled the Ranger.

No hints he tried drew Turk out as to their destination, and what they meant to do when they reached it. He could only follow along, and hope to divert the ferocious Crimson Riders when he discovered what Turk and Farney were up to.

They pulled up, an hour before night fell, to rest the horses, and to eat and drink. When dark came over the wilderness, the order was given to get ready. The steers were closely guarded by expert handlers.

Mariscal proved to be their objective. In the night, the large band of heavily armed Riders approached the little settlement. The drovers ran the bunch of KO steers off to the east, pulling them around and checking them not far from the village gates, which had been closed at dark.

Turk Monroe, with his fighting men, approached the gates. Several lariats whipped out, settling over the sharp tops of the palings, and the horsemen whirled and rode hard, jerking the gates with them. Shouts of alarm came from inside, and a gun blazed.

The attack was on!

The gates crashed pulling a section of the thorn-studded fence along, as the Crimson Riders spurred their mustangs and galloped off, leaving a large gap through which their companions could ride.

Jim Hatfield was caught in the crush of savage, heavily armed men, the Crimson Riders he was spying upon and hoped to crush himself. Turk Monroe was in the thick of it all, bellowing his commands. Farney, well to the rear, watched as his men did their cruel work. He twirled the end of his mustache with thumb and forefinger as he sat his horse and observed the raid on the little settlement.

Shrill whistle signals, and the Riders holding the KO steers began hazing the big animals to the opening, to drive them through.

"Come on, boys!" howled Turk, brandishing his six-shooter. "In and at 'em! Drive 'em inside and shoot any who show!"

A Mexican in a serape and a steeple sombrero, a gate guard, was screeching the alarm at the top of his voice.

"Bandidos!" he shrilled, over and over, and fired a shot at the attackers.

Colts, shotguns and carbines flamed and the sentry died in his tracks.

There were lights on in the Contreras *hacienda* and in several of the shacks but many who lived in the village had turned in. The harsh cries of the Crimson Riders, the banging guns, the pounding hoofs that shook the earth, startled the sleepers to sudden alarm. Peons and *vaqueros* rushed from their huts, followed by sleepy-eyed children and women, astounded at the night raid.

"Inside or yuh die!" howled Turk Monroe, his pistols going at full speed.

Seizing their children, women began to scream as they sought shelter in the brush-walled houses, or behind adobe walls. A few answering shots came at the Riders but the resistance was not organized. Swift reprisal followed any attempt at defense, bunches of Turk's gang pouring lead into any man who dared show himself.

Swept along in the van, on the golden sorrel, the Ranger gritted his teeth, desperate because he was unable to check the terrible assault. Innocent people were dying, and the cries of the wounded joined in the bloody aura that rose over the unfortunate little town.

Turk Monroe, his cohorts spreading out to subdue the place, drove on to the *hacienda*, closely surrounded by his closest aides, Blackie, Moon, Jack, Fats, and the supposed Jim Howes. The front door opened and Luis Contreras stood there, his fowling-piece in his hands.

"Drop that gun, Contreras!" bellowed Turk, taking aim. "It's the Law! Yuh're under arrest!"

"Who is eet — what do you do?" shouted Contreras, his face red in the light.

Colonel Farney galloped in, and brought his black gelding to a sliding stop. His voice had a commanding ring, carrying over the din as he addressed the don.

"Contreras, the Crimson Flower has come to exact retribution from your people! You are guilty of stealing cattle and shooting decent cowmen on this range. I'll give you just five minutes to surrender the village. If a single shot is fired at us after that, we will destroy every man and burn the settlement!"

Contreras heard Farney clearly. Taken aback, the proud don quickly realized the danger to his people. They were already defeated, and there were women, children and old folks to protect. The don sought to parley, to temporize.

"Senor, who are you?" he called. "What's the meaning of thees?"

"You're losing time, Contreras," warned Farney. "Drop that shotgun. You're covered from a dozen angles! Pronto!"

In the lighted doorway, the don realized he would die. He would leave his women, his friends, to a horrible fate. His bearded face worked, as he was forced to make his unhappy decision. Scattered firing still rang out, as here and there a *vaquero,* barricaded in his hut, fought it out.

"We are the Law here," went on the chief of the Crimson Riders. "And you are in the wrong!"

Luis Contreras was a brave man. Alone, he might have chosen to die, rather than surrender. But there were many others to consider.

"And if I surrender?" he called.

"Then you and your people will live."

"You only got three minutes left, Contreras!" sang out Turk Monroe.

Contreras threw his weapon to the ground and, folding his arms, coolly stepped out to face his enemies.

"Ver-ee well, senores," he said. "What am I to do?"

"First," ordered Farney, "tell your men to quit firing on us."

Contreras, his slim figure stiffly erect, walked forth. He called out to his friends in Spanish, telling them to stop the hopeless resistance. Farney and Monroe, their guns ready to kill, followed the don on their horses through the dirt ways. Riders with the red flower shining on shirt fronts, and with weapons handy, were all through the town. Frightened eyes peeked from windows.

The Mexicans obeyed their leader, and when he had checked their resistance, Contreras turned to look up again at Farney. His bearded lips were grim, and his dark eyes burned with rage, but he kept his self-control.

"And now, senor, will you please to explain why you hav' done thees to innocent ceetizens," he said calmly. "We are not thieves and keelers!"

"Don't stand there and try to tell me you don't know what's been goin' on in your own village!" growled Farney, his waxed mustache jumping. "We've secretly watched you for a long time, and we've caught you red-handed!"

"What do you mean, senor?" asked the don.

Farney shrugged. "All right — if you want me to prove it! Step over there to your pens!"

At the south side of the enclosure, a wooden fence had been constructed, and into this corral horses, goats and cows could be held overnight. Urged by Farney, Don Luis walked to the pens. Excited animals still milled about, but they were quieting somewhat since the firing and shouts had stopped.

"Let's have some light on the subject, Turk," said Farney.

Monroe's men carried burlap bags with pitch torches in them. Several were lighted, giving a ruby illumination to the scene. Farney pointed at several big steers near the fence.

"Will you please read that brand for me, Contreras?" he said sneeringly.

"KO — ees Pierce's brand!" Don Luis blinked, hardly able to believe his eyes.

"That shows yuh can read," drawled Monroe.

"Senor Far-ney, those cows were not zere at sundown!" Contreras cried. "I do not savvy how zey came here."

"Stop lying," snapped Farney.

Hatfield, close to Turk Monroe, was furious, his rage icy cold. The Riders had driven some of Pierce's steers down with them, and had hazed them into the pens! Now Farney was accusing the Mexicans of rustling them.

"We'll go back to your *hacienda*," said Farney, "and talk it over, Contreras. My organization is being paid to protect this range from scum like you. Your Mexicans have been stealin' regularly from the Texans."

Contreras, helpless, and covered by the Crimson Riders' guns, shrugged and walked back to his home.

"Luis — Luis!"

His wife ran to throw her arms about the don's neck, as Contreras, head up, stepped into the great room in which Hatfield had seen Jerry Addison with the don and his family. Teresa stood to one side. She wore a black silk dress, and her beauty had never been more striking.

CHAPTER IX
SHAKE-DOWN

Farney, following Contreras in, saw the pretty Mexican girl. He ogled her, bowed from the waist, twirled his mustache.

"Senorita, a pleasure!" he said. "Hem-hem!" Farney cleared his throat in his characteristic way.

Turk Monroe, standing in the wide entry with Hatfield and Blackie, nudged the Ranger.

"The colonel's a great hand with the ladies!" he whispered. "He's mighty elergant, ain't he? A great hombre!"

"Oh, yes — a sure enough swell!" muttered the Ranger.

He leaned against the door frame, watching the unhappy scene. And outside the Crimson Riders swarmed in the village, trigger fingers itching.

"Rosa," Don Luis ordered his wife sternly. "Take Teresa to her rooms! I am not hurt."

Farney's quick eyes swept the gold and

silver ornaments in the large, low-ceilinged living room. The eyes narrowed, as his lips twitched. He drew in his breath sharply.

Senorita Contreras and her mother had left, going to their apartments in another part of the *hacienda.* Contreras faced his tormentors alone. His hands were shaking but it was not because of fear. He was furiously angry.

"There ees meestake somewhere, Senor el Colonel," he said. "But what ees eet you want?"

Farney stepped to the sideboard. He poured himself a drink from a beautiful silver decanter standing on a heavy, hand-beaten silver tray. His fingers lingered on the metal carvings as he admired the valuable collection.

"Lovely things here, Don Luis," he remarked. "I have a passion for such — but we'll discuss the business. You and your people are in a bad situation. I've caught you red-handed. Several men have been shot and killed by the rustlers. You're a friend of Chihuahua Pete's, the notorious outlaw, aren't you? Givin' him a hiding-place when he needs it?"

Contreras shook his head. He folded his arms, watching Farney, waiting.

"It's not the habit of my organization,"

frowned Farney, "to waste time calling in the Law. Too many slips between arrest and justice, Contreras. Across the Pecos here there's not much law, anyway, so we must take care of ourselves. That's what the Crimson Flower is for. So it's up to me what your punishment shall be. You understand?"

"Perfectly," replied Contreras softly.

"You have women and children here," Farney went on. "We don't want to fight them. But your *vaqueros* have stolen cattle off the range, and you must pay for the damage so we can recompense the ranchers you've robbed. If you are willing to make reparation, then we won't punish the village further. But if you refuse, or if you seek revenge against us, by Jupiter, my Riders will be down on you and wipe out every livin' soul here!"

Farney was serious. In his voice was a harsh threat.

"I believe you," said Don Luis. "Tell me now, what do you want, senor?"

"You have some things of value right here in this room, perhaps enough to pay for the material damages you and your people have done," suggested Farney. "I will turn them into cash and pay Pierce and the others for the loss of their cattle. You refuse to tell me where I can find Chihuahua Pete?"

"I do not refuse, but I cannot," replied Contreras quietly.

The don was no fool. Jim Hatfield could see that he understood why Farney had come. But he also understood the savagery of the Crimson Riders, and he was determined to save as many lives of his people as possible.

"Very well," Farney said. "I'll come up with those rustlers later, and attend to them. As to you, I am going to pick out what I think will be enough, and take the things with me. You're agreeable?"

"What else can I be, senor?" A faint smile touched the don's lips.

"Hem-hem." Farney cleared his throat again. "Turk, have the boys empty that big chest in the corner," he ordered.

"You Howes — Blackie," said Monroe. "Let's go."

They tossed the linen that filled the chest on the floor, and Farney began picking out what he fancied from the large collection — gold and silver urns, platters and figurines, crucifixes and strings of golden beads. He caressed them, gloating over their loveliness. But he kept an eye on his men, also.

"Take care there, you," he said sharply to Hatfield, as the Ranger placed a large golden pitcher in the chest. "Don't dent anything. Better pack some of those napkins between 'em, so they won't be scratched."

When the big chest had been filled, with Farney taking most of the valuables in the room, the Crimson Flower leader again approached Contreras.

"You'll write out a bill-of-sale, Contreras," he said, "saying you've received payment for these treasures."

Don Luis went to his desk. He wrote as Farney directed, with a golden penholder which held a quill pen. When Don Luis had finished, Farney placed the penholder in his pocket.

"Very good." He nodded. "Now I'll give you one final word of warning, Don Luis. Keep quiet about what happened here tonight. If you don't, I'll be back, and you won't get off so easily."

"Si — si," the don said wearily. "Now, if you hav' feeneesh, will you go?"

"Get hold, there, Howes," ordered Turk.

Blackie had one handle of the chest. It was heavy, filled with the gold and silver objects.

"Careful how you tote it, boys," cautioned Turk. "Take it out and tie it on one of them mules from the corral."

Hatfield, biding his time until it was possible for him to take some action, obeyed.

He and Blackie started out the front door with the treasure. Farney poured himself another drink.

"Good evening, Don Luis," Farney said, when he had downed the drink. "We will go now, since you've made reparation."

"In my language," said Contreras smoothly, unable to resist a parting shot, "we have anuzzer name for it, Senor el Colonel. We call it stealing!"

Farney's face reddened. He twirled his mustache, and stepped closer to Don Luis.

"You dirty little monkey," he said viciously. "Remember my warnin'!"

Farney struck, hard, hitting Contreras in the mouth, splitting the don's lip against his teeth. Blood spurted, and the slim don staggered back. But, infuriated beyond control by the blow, Don Luis leaped at Farney, slashing at him with his fists. Before he could do much damage, though, Turk Monroe seized the don from behind, jerking back his head, throttling him.

Contreras fell, and Farney, with Turk assisting, began to kick Contreras, swearing at him, beating him until he lost consciousness and lay quiet on the floor. . . .

The next afternoon, following that dread night when the thieves and killers who had invaded Mariscal had disappeared through the darkness with their loot, on the same range a young rider was heading happily toward the town, with nothing to warn him of the devastation that had struck.

Jerry Addison was busy with pleasing thoughts as he rode toward Mariscal. He was going to call on Teresa Contreras, the little senorita with whom he had fallen so deeply in love. After he had glimpsed Teresa that first time, he had been unable to shake off the memory of her lovely face, the beautiful, startled eyes that had met his for a magic moment.

So a day or so later he had approached the settlement, and the friendly Mexicans, after he had told them who he was, had taken him to Don Luis. A fine gentleman, Contreras had liked the bronc buster from the start. He had soon introduced Jerry to his family, to Senora Contreras and to the daughter, Teresa.

From that time, Addison had spent a great deal of time near Mariscal. He had finished up with most of K. O. Pierce's mustangs at the ranch, and his work of catching the wild horses provided an excellent excuse for him to ride off alone.

During the days, Addison was constructing runs and a trap to catch the mustangs. But in the evenings he could ride down to visit with Teresa and her parents, and be back at his camp near Elephant Knob in plenty of time for sufficient sleep. After a visit or two, the hospitable Mexicans had insisted that he spend the night at the *hacienda*. Addison had already stayed there twice.

"Mebbe I'll stay tonight, if they ask me," he decided, speaking his thoughts aloud. "Ain't she a beauty, though, Blue?"

He often talked to his horse, and voiced his ideas even though he happened to be alone. He rode the range in solitary splendor much of the time, and the habit had become ingrained. But Addison didn't mind being alone on the range. He liked being independent, and prided himself on being able to take care of himself.

"But, Blue," he murmured, "if Teresa throwed a halter on me, I reckon I wouldn't try to duck out of it, the way you do some cold mornin's when yuh feel frisky! Fact is, I'll jump right into it."

It was fortunate for Addison, though he would not have thought so, that the attack on Mariscal by Farney and his Crimson Riders had taken place on a night when the bronc buster had not been in the Mexican village.

But he was quite unaware that anything

had happened there as he approached the town and sang out when he came to the gates. He noticed that a section of the palings, topped with thorned brush, was propped up, as though it had fallen down and been hastily mended, but thought nothing of it.

The afternoon was warm and a hazy, almost dusty cloak lay on the dry land. Butterflies, and other insects buzzed lazily about the flowers, and over the village.

There was no delay in letting Addison through. The gate was opened and a sleepy-eyed peon waved him past. They all knew him well, as Don Luis' friend.

Naked brown children were playing among the kids, pigs and chickens in the dust. There were women around, at work or gossiping, but Addison thought the place quieter than usual.

He rode Blue directly to the *hacienda,* saw to it that his horse was taken care of, and left in the shade, then went to the open front door.

Contreras met him, greeted him.

"Why, Don Luis!" exclaimed Addison. "What hit yuh!"

The don's face was grim. It was also swollen, and his lips were cut and enlarged. One eye was almost closed, and there were fresh scabs on his face. He carried his left arm in a sling, a silk kerchief rigged around his neck.

"*Amigo mio,* you are welcome here, as always!" he cried. "You ask what hit me? Last night there was trouble. We had a veesit from the Crimson Ridaires, *si.*"

"The Riders!" Addison checked a curse. "What'd they do to yuh?"

Don Luis shrugged. "This," he said, "and worse. Three people were keeled, and several more wounded by flying bullets. Also, zey robbed me, but that's unimportant, compared to the friends who were shot."

The big sideboard and refectory table were almost bare. All the valuable gold and silver plate had disappeared. Bit by bit, from Don Luis, and from Senora Contreras and Teresa, young Addison learned of the raid by Farney and his men.

The bronc buster was infuriated as he listened. He gritted his teeth and his fingers worked.

"I wish I'd been here!" he exclaimed. "They wouldn't have got off so easy!"

"You would have die', my boy," said Don Luis. "I'm glad you were not here. Zere were too man-ee of zem."

"This is the rawest thing I ever heard of!" exclaimed Addison. "I'm goin' to take it up right away with Pierce!"

"Pierce?" said Don Luis, with an expressive shrug. "Why, Senor Pierce hires the Ridaires! I was surprise' not to see heem, too. His cowboys hav' fire' on my *vaqueros,* but I hav' geeven ordaires to my friends not to fight back but to ride away."

Addison knew how Contreras felt, for he knew that one bullet would bring a dozen retaliatory ones, in the dangerous situation existing. Only a spark was needed to ignite a conflagration, to start a bloody war to the death between the ranchers to the north and the people of Mariscal. Don Luis understandably wished to avoid such a feud.

"K. O. Pierce is an honest man," Addison said slowly. "He might gun you or anybody he believed stole his cattle — and some are right sure that Chihuahua Pete and his men run down this way and get help from the villagers. But Pierce would never rob yuh, the way Farney did. I'm goin' to tell him about it."

Contreras put a hand on the young man's arm.

"No, please," he said earnestly. "I can stand the loss of my treas-ures. What I fear is that Farney weel come back and keel more of my friends. So he threaten', eef we talk too much, if we tell what happened last night."

"Why, Farney and his gang ain't no better than outlaws!" growled Addison.

He was burning with rage, against the unfairness of it, the terrible injustice. Where could he get help, allies strong enough to crush the Crimson Riders? For they must be destroyed.

What Contreras said of K. O. Pierce and the Anglo-Saxon element on the range was quite true. Addison had heard talk against the Spanish-Americans of Mariscal. Where did Chihuahua Pete come in?

In familiarizing himself with the terrain around Elephant Knob, in order to trap the mustangs which had gone wild, Addison had come upon myriad crisscrossing animal trails, of cattle and horses, of deer and mountain lions. There had been a few signs of that most dangerous creature, man. In a dry arroyo through which he had been riding, he had picked up one of the red flower badges sported by Farney's organization.

Snooping around, he had finally located a cavern where the remains of cookfires, and other evidence, told him that men had camped. Not wishing to disturb anything and so alarm whoever was using it as a hiding-place, he had carefully covered his tracks and decided to watch the cave.

And, four days ago, while moving near Elephant Knob, he had been fired upon by drygulchers. He was sure the bullets had come from near that secret camp. A flash of sunlight on a gun barrel had warned him, perhaps saved his life.

He turned over all the evidence he had against the Crimson Riders. Contreras' story made them out-and-out bandits. Farney had said he meant to use the stolen goods as reparations to pay K. O. Pierce and the other ranchers for their lost cattle.

"If Pierce savvies of this raid, and takes his share," he thought, "that means I'm through with him. He's no better'n Farney."

But there was a good chance that Farney had lied, and meant to keep the treasures for himself.

"I'll find out for shore," Addison decided firmly, "and I'll find out right about Farney and his bunch. Then I'll take the whole thing and drop it in Pierce's lap. If he won't help down Farney's gang, then I'll hunt other men who will! The Rangers, mebbe."

CHAPTER X
CAPTURED

Young Addison spent an hour with his friends in Mariscal. Teresa was fearful, after what had occurred, and begged him to take care of himself when he rode through the wilds.

After supper, Jerry took his leave of his friends in Mariscal, on the plea that his work would make it necessary for him to get to his camp in time to get plenty of sleep. He would not alarm them further by telling them what he actually meant to do.

Hitting the trail on Blue, Addison headed straight for Big Bend, the little crossroads town where he knew that Colonel Bartholomew Farney had his headquarters. He was mad clean through at the Crimson Riders and their kind, and swore as he rode.

"I'll pick up all I can at Big Bend," he muttered, "and then head to the KO and have it out with Pierce."

It was a long run to the little town. But

Addison had come through it on his way to KO, so he knew the lay of the land. The gray of dawn was touching the eastern sky, as the bronc buster on the dusty and tired Blue, approached Big Bend.

"We'll lie up and rest through the day, Blue," he promised. "Then we'll see what's what tonight."

He turned east, and made some high ground on the other side of Big Bend, a ridge in a series running roughly east and west. The ridges were heavily bushed, and offered plenty of hiding places. Addison unsaddled Blue and hobbled the horse. Then, taking his rifle and his binoculars — he often used the field-glasses in his work to locate bands of wild horses — he moved to the western bluff of the ridge he had picked.

It made a good observation point. He could lie in the sandy soil on the end of the ridge. There, screened by thick chaparral, he watched the enemy stronghold through-out the day. He had a great stock of patience for he had learned that by handling horses.

The Crimson Riders were late risers, he discovered. With his glasses focused and the lenses kept hidden from the sun, so that those below would not get a telltale flash, Addison observed the man as they ate breakfast, and lounged about.

A few pairs of them played horseshoes. Others haunted the Mexican's saloon. Horsemen went out, but soon returned, as though exercising themselves and their mounts, and men practised with their six-shooters, using cans from the piles behind the store and *cantina* as targets.

"They're takin' it easy today," decided Addison.

He could recognize many of them. Turk Monroe's gangling figure was easy to iden-tify when he left the headquarters office and went to the saloon, or to the long carriage shed which served as a barracks for the rank and file of the Crimson Riders.

Addison also knew Blackie and Moon, for he had met them at the KO. And he watched for a time the big recruit — Jim Somebody, it was. Jerry's keen memory retained details, and he recalled seeing the tall man with Turk, Blackie and his bunch at the KO.

In the afternoon, he spied Colonel Far-ney, who emerged from his headquarters, and mounted a black gelding with a single white stocking on his foreleg. Farney, spick-and-span as usual, rode off westward on the black. Addison did not see the man return, while the daylight lasted.

He took a nap when dark fell, to give the

men below time to settle down for the night. It was close to twelve o'clock before he roused, picked up Blue, saddled his horse, and rode toward Big Bend.

Well out from the town, he stopped at a thicket on a rise, which he had picked during the day. He dropped his reins, and tied his bandanna carefully about Blue's muzzle, for the horse was apt to nicker when he heard or scented the approach of the man who rode him.

Afoot, Addison dodged toward the buildings which loomed against the sky. The moon had risen, and the shadows were long.

He rubbed some dirt on his face and hands, a usual precaution against gleaming skies in the darkness. He moved stealthily, flitting from spot to spot of cover, on a route predetermined by his observations. He avoided the carriage shed, where the Riders slept. Their horses were turned out on hobbles, or held in a big corral to the rear.

Headquarters was Addison's chief objective. He wanted to find out, if possible, whether Farney had the things there — the treasures he had stolen from Don Luis Contreras. He hoped, too, that he might overhear something.

But there was no light on anywhere in town save at the saloon, where a few candles were flickering. The saloon door stood open and he could see inside. Turk Monroe, Blackie Moon and the big recruit, Jim — he had it now, it was Jim Howes — were sitting at a table, still drinking.

"Reckon Farney ain't come back tonight," thought the bronc buster. "Mebbe he went to Pierce's or Young's!"

It was his chance. He sneaked on past the saloon and, lying flat out from the building which was the Riders' headquarters, began to worm his way in toward Farney's office. He got in safely, on the dark side of the structure. The front door was closed, but he was right under a window which was open.

Ears wide, the alert bronc buster was unable to hear anything in the office.

It was a golden opportunity, he thought. If he could find just where Colonel Farney had placed Don Luis' property, that evidence would go a long way toward proving the Crimson Riders' guilt for the benefit of K.O. Pierce, the Law, and others. On Addison's information, knowing just where the antique treasures were, Pierce could make a raid.

Jerry Addison straightened up, and peeked into the office. The only light that he had was a streamer of moonlight coming in through an opposite window. There were vague sounds of voices and laughter from the *cantina* down the way, but the headquarters seemed deserted. Addison pulled himself up and slid over the sill.

His heart beat like a trip-hammer from the excitement. He was taking a big gamble, staking his life against the clinching evidence he hoped to procure. But he was mad at the Riders all the way through, and he wanted to help Teresa's father, his friends, the people of Mariscal. But if caught, he was certain that he would be killed.

Crouched inside, he sought to orient himself. The bulk of a desk stood at his left. There were several chairs, a mat, and the front entry was behind him. He kept low as he moved around. There were two closed doors at the rear of the room. He listened at both, but they were dark and not a sound came from behind either.

Returning to his investigation, he came upon a wooden chest in a corner. It had a padlock on it. Carefully, Addison hefted it. It was very heavy.

"It could hold all that stuff," he thought, growing hopeful. Yet if he broke the padlock, it would tell them a spy had been there.

Squatted at one end of the chest, he tried to decide what he should do. He hefted it again, scarcely able to raise one end off the board floor. The contents shifted a bit, and he caught a faint metallic tinkle. The things stolen from Mariscal were chiefly of good size. They would have rolled, made a different sort of noise. His flared nostrils picked up a faint odor of gunpowder.

"Cartridges!" he thought.

He was more disappointed than if he had not come upon the locked chest. He did not need to open it now, to be sure it was not the treasure.

Growing bolder as he made his tour without any alarm, Addison crept to the left-hand door at the rear of the office. He was convinced that Colonel Farney, whom he had seen ride away that afternoon, was not in Big Bend. And Turk Monroe was over at the saloon.

The door had a latch, and his deft fingers touched the lift. It came up quietly, and he opened the door softly, with but a slight creak or two of leather hinges. Looking in, he saw that the room was a small one, with a single window. He could make out a bunk, a chair and a table on which a couple of empty whisky bottles stood. In the back was a half-open door, leading outside to where the moonlight was bright.

There was nothing to interest Addison in the small room. He went back into the office, and tried the second door. But this was bolted from the other side.

He hesitated; then he went stealthily through the smaller room and out the back way. Sure enough, he found that the larger room had its own exit, and the door was open to the warm night.

This set his mind at rest as to the bolted door. The occupants of these rear rooms could come and go by the back ways.

"That one must be Farney's!" he decided.

He had convinced himself that Farney was away from Big Bend and, hearing nothing inside the bedroom, he stepped through the door. It was darker inside than out. But the room had three windows, two at the side, and the other a small aperture at the right of the back door.

The moonlight coming in glinted on metal. He glided over and stood before a flat-topped table against the partition separating the two sleeping-rooms. It held, in plain sight, just what he had been searching for. He was certain of it, though the light was none too good. There were metal vases, urns, pitchers, and golden trays.

"This is it!" he gloated. "I've found it! Farney's mighty shore of hisself, leavin' it out in plain sight!"

"Beautiful, aren't they?" suddenly said a

cold voice from behind him.

Addison jumped so violently that his feet left the mat. He wanted to whirl and fight, but a stabbing beam from a bull's-eye lantern, the slide quickly opened, caught him, outlining him clearly for whoever had spoken. He was not sure just where the voice had come from.

"I have you covered with a shotgun, and both barrels are loaded with buck," remarked the cold, unpleasant voice. "It'll tear you to shreds if I pull the trigger . . . Drop your pistol. Drop it, pronto!"

Blinded by the bull's-eye, Addison thought desperately of firing at the light, in the hope of hitting his enemy. As though divining his plan, the man said:

"I'm not behind the light. I moved as soon as I opened the slide."

Cold sweat stood out on the bronc buster. The instant to throw himself flat and fire wildly with the hope of hitting his captor had passed. Now he must try to temporize, talk his way out of the danger he was in. His fingers relaxed, and his Colt clanked on the floor as he put up his hands.

"I'm sorry, mister," he said, finding his voice. "Is this where Turk has his bunk? He asked me to step over and pick up somethin' for him — his poncho."

A faint laugh answered this lame attempt of Addison's to explain his presence. Eyes growing accustomed to the bull's-eye, Jerry could see who it was who had laughed. Colonel Bartholomew Farney was covering him with a sawed-off, double-barreled shotgun.

The chief of the Crimson Riders had on a pair of brown trousers, his feet were bare, and he wore a silk shirt, open at the neck. He had been lying in his bunk. A chair beside the bunk held the lantern, but Farney himself had moved to the other end of the room, from which vantage point he could watch the intruder with little danger to himself, in case Addison had tried firing at the bull's-eye.

"Hem-hem!" Farney cleared his throat. He peered over at the bronc buster. "Why, it's Addison, the mustanger, isn't it? This is a surprise. When I first heard you in the next room I thought it was Turk coming in. Then when you sneaked in here, I decided it was one of our own men, his larcenous soul getting the better of him. I wouldn't put it past some of 'em to try and steal those beautiful bits of art. They do arouse cupidity, don't they? I suppose you couldn't resist trying to take some for yourself?"

Farney was talking, to draw him out,

Addison knew, and he regained his aplomb as the first fright at being caught abated.

"I ain't here to steal, Farney," he drawled, and he was unable to keep the contempt from his voice.

But he wondered at his rashness in coming here alone to the Crimson Riders' stronghold. It had seemed feasible, when he had attempted it. But trapped under the gun, he knew how foolhardy he had been.

"Aren't you?" said Farney. "You'd have a hard time making anyone believe that, sir. Hem-hem."

The dark eyes of the shotgun pinned Addison. As Farney had said, the buck would rip him to shreds at such range.

"On the other hand," continued Farney, enjoying his sadistic role, "I do believe you! Now that I know who you are, I think you came to spy on me. Is that right?"

Addison shrugged. He held his hands shoulder-high.

Farney kept talking, evidently trying to draw him. "I know that you are in love with Contreras' daughter. The don sent you to recover his treasures, perhaps to kill me!"

"That ain't true!" Addison was prodded into protesting. If Farney thought Contreras had sent him, it would send the Crimson Riders back on Mariscal, to raid and burn and kill. "I'm here on my own. Don Luis told me yuh'd killed his friends and robbed him, but he begged me not to talk of it or do anything to rile yuh. Contreras has nothin' to do with me bein' here, savvy? It's my own idea."

"Hem-hem!" Farney was laughing at him, his waxed mustache jumping, his white teeth gleaming. "Love forces a man to do silly things. Imagine an ignorant young fellow such as you daring to mix it and match wits with me! Well, I warned Contreras not to talk. Since he's disobeyed me, I'll have to exact further retribution and pay Mariscal another visit. What did Pierce say, when you told him?"

"I didn't tell anybody —"

Jerry Addison broke off. He was chagrined, as he realized that Farney had been twisting the knife in the wound, gaining information from him. He had admitted that he had come alone. His anger at Farney and his Riders, contained so long, boiled over in his irritation.

"You lobo, Farney!" he cried. "The rope's too good for yore neck! But yuh'll stretch it, and mighty soon. The law'll take care of you and yore outlaw riders! I savvy plenty about yuh, and yuh'll be caught up with before long. Yuh're a bunch of robbers! This whole

Crimson Rider set-up is to shake down the ranchers — and worse!"

"That's better," said Farney with ominous quiet. He had stopped smiling. "At least we know where we stand." He called, without taking his eyes off Addison, "Turk — Blackie! This way."

The saloon stood a few doors down, and Farney's strong voice carried in the night to the men inside.

Hurrying steps sounded, and Turk Monroe, followed by Blackie, Moon and Jim Howes, dashed to Farney's door.

"Come in," ordered Farney, as his minions arrived. "I have a pleasant surprise for you, Turk."

Monroe's gangling figure paused in the doorway. He stared at the captive. Then his crooked smile came to his lips.

"Well, dog my hide if it ain't the young bronc buster!"

Chapter XI
The Fight at Big Bend

Jim Hatfield stared over Turk's shoulder into Colonel Farney's room. The Ranger was appalled as he recognized the prisoner Farney was holding there.

"Watch him, Turk," ordered Farney.

He placed his shotgun in the corner, and going over to the chair beside his bunk, removed the cap from the bull's-eye so that the light became general in the room. It shone on the gold and silver trinkets which had been stolen from Don Luis in Mariscal, and showed the colonel's clothing, hung on pegs, as well as papers and other belongings about the place.

"How in tarnation blazes did yuh catch the young fool, Boss?" asked Turk.

"I heard someone in your room, Turk," explained Farney. "At first I thought it might be you and didn't investigate. Then he actually sneaked in here, and I watched him. He was after the things on the table."

"I savvy," gloated Turk, stepping closer to Addison. " 'Won't you walk into my parlor, said the spider to the fly!' Reminds me of the one about the feller who swiped some cows from the I C brand. He jist adds a 'U', makin' it 'I C U.' So the owner took 'em back and adds another figger, makin' it 'I C U2!' "

Blackie, Moon and Howes chuckled, and Farney smiled.

"Always ready with a gay little jest, eh, Turk?" said the chief of the Crimson Riders. "In this case, though, the joke's on Addison. No wonder he looks so glum."

Turk's crooked smile showed his big yellow teeth. He struck out, hitting Jerry Addison in the face with the flat of his hand.

"You polecat!" he growled. "I got plenty to C U about! Yuh been spyin' on us. We savvy yuh been snoopin' around our cave down near Elephant Knob! Fact is, we know all about yuh. I just been waitin' for a chance to give yuh what yuh've asked for!"

Addison, recoiling from the blow, started back, his hands flying down, clenching. But he bit his lip, for all these men were armed, and besides he was helplessly outnumbered.

"From what I can gather," said Farney coolly, "no one knows he came here, Turk." He yawned. "Go on and get it over with. I want to get some sleep tonight. You can plant him out in the bush."

Hatfield was racking his brain for some way to save Jerry Addison, whose temerity in coming to Big Bend had resulted in this tragic climax. As Monroe, unwilling to forego the pleasure of tormenting the prisoner, swore and railed at Addison, the big Ranger hunted for a method of getting Jerry out of the scrape.

Only too well Hatfield knew that the bronc buster faced death, and soon. Monroe hated Addison, and had only been awaiting the chance to kill him.

Hatfield had gathered damning evidence against the Crimson Riders. He knew them all, most of them by name, as well as the leaders. He had seen them raid and kill at Mariscal. He was aware of Farney's ambition to spread the "protective society" throughout Texas, until Farney grew so powerful that nothing could check his career. Turk had hinted that the colonel had political ambitions, and was making contacts. As the Crimson Riders gained momentum they would prove harder and harder to stop.

One angle had kept Hatfield with them for a few more days than he had intended to be. He wanted to discover how Chihuahua Pete, the big Mexican rustler, fitted into the picture. He had a hunch that perhaps Chihuahua Pete had connections with Farney. At the hidden camp near Elephant Knob, he had been given a hint that signals would bring confederates to the cave. Lenihan, mentioned by Turk and Moon, had been the name of a go-between, and perhaps the link between the Mexican raiders and the Crimson Riders.

There were gaps in this, however, which the thorough-going Ranger had wished to fill in to his satisfaction, for the purposes of arresting the outlaws. After the Mariscal raid, they had been taking it easy for a time, but Monroe had told him they would soon be riding out for "real sport."

The recruit would see something mighty cute, Turk had promised. So Hatfield had bided his time.

"We're goin' to kill yuh, Addison," he heard Monroe saying now. "Mebbe I'll make it so's yuh'll die slow-like. Shoot yuh in the middle. How'd yuh like that? Sorry, how's that little senorita kiss? Sweet as a calf, I'll bet! Mebbe I'll call on her myself with you out of the way!"

Addison trembled with fury. "Leave her out of it, Turk. If yuh touch her, I'll — I'll kill yuh for it!"

Turk's vile tongue lashed the bronc buster. He had found a way to torture Addison, one that was worse than physical pain, and he made the most of it. Addison's face was burning, red as fire. He clenched his fists, bit his lip, as Monroe talked on about Teresa.

Farney was amused, too. He twirled his mustache, and his bright eyes shone.

"You make the little senorita sound delicious, Turk," he said. "Perhaps I'll cut the cards with you for who will court her next!"

Blackie was grinning, and so was the huge, stupid Moon, as Monroe sought to egg the helpless prisoner into a false move. They meant to kill Addison, and soon. It was only a matter of how Turk did it.

Perhaps Monroe wished to force Addison to strike at him. Then Farney's field chief could show off the swiftness of his gun draw. Turk's smooth-handled, pet Colt rode in his right-hand holster, ready to go.

Jerry Addison broke suddenly. With a wild cry, he lunged in and struck at Monroe.

It was as Hatfield had thought. Turk wanted to show how fast he was. Monroe jumped back, and his hand fled to his Colt, but stopped on the butt as Hatfield's voice said sharply: "Hold it! Freeze, everybody!"

The Ranger revolver was out, hammer

spur back under a long thumb. Hatfield, in the doorway, covered them.

Astounded, they took their eyes off Addison, staring at the tall man.

"I ain't goin' to shoot, boys," drawled the Ranger, "unless yuh make me. All I want is for Addison to get free. . . . This way, bronc buster."

A sudden, unbelieving light sprang to Jerry Addison's face. His eyes widened, and he obeyed with alacrity.

"Yuh fool, Howes!" Turk yelled angrily. "That *tequila* must've gone to yore head! Don't yuh savvy what yuh're doin'?"

"I'm takin' Addison out of here alive, Turk," Hatfield said coldly.

So stunned were the Crimson Riders at the supposed recruit's treachery that Addison was almost at the door before they began to recover from the shock.

"This'll cost yuh dear, Howes," snarled Farney. All he could do was snarl, for his shotgun was several feet away, in the corner.

"Come on, Jim, a joke's a joke," growled Turk. "Put up yore gun and we'll forget it. You savvy Addison's our enemy."

Blackie, the squat, bearded plug-ugly who had been Hatfield's constant nurse since the Ranger had joined the Riders, stood at Hatfield's right hand. As Addison, in his hurry to escape from the death trap, ducked between Blackie and the tall officer in the door, Blackie went for his Colt, sure he could win in the fraction of a second he had.

Blackie made a good try. He was fast, and had practised until he was all but perfect with a six-shooter. His .45 Colt cleared the oiled holster, rose with the flash of his hand — and Hatfield had to fire within inches of Jerry Addison's slim body to save the bronc buster and himself.

The Ranger pistol blared; it spat smoke and lead, as Hatfield raised his thumb from the hammer spur. Blackie's weapon roared as the plug-ugly took a slug in the heart. Addison lurched forward. Blackie's bullet had cut his boot top and lodged in the sill between the Ranger's spread feet.

Blackie was done. He had been leaning forward when the slug caught him and now he kept going, falling on his face.

Turk Monroe, with a shrill yelp, dived to one side. He kicked at the chair holding the lantern, and it crashed to the floor, went out. Farney, too, had ducked, seizing the breath of time it took Hatfield to dispose of Blackie.

Addison righted himself, and turned, his weight on his right leg.

"Come on, mister!" he gasped. "We better

get!" He would not leave without his res-
cuer.

"Run for yore hoss, Addison — pronto!"
ordered Hatfield.

He jumped to one side knocking Addison
out of the direct line of the door. A huge
figure loomed there — Moon, trying to
make a hero out of himself before Farney
and Turk. Moon's gun blazed, but the bullets were wild.

"Out of the way, yuh big lummox!"
shrieked Turk, for Moon was blocking the
doorway.

Farney had his shotgun now. Buck would
spread, perhaps stop the escaping men as
they ran away.

Hatfield's bullets, directed at the dark
rectangle of Farney's back door, brought a
cry of pain from Moon. All the men were
cursing and yelling. And from the carriage
shed ran dark figures of other Crimson Riders, reinforcements for Farney and Turk.

Shrill whistles issued from the tall officer's
lips. They penetrated the din, over the
frantic shouts of Turk Monroe as he bellowed to his killers. Hatfield was moving,
half turned and with his Colt up, so he
could cover that open door behind which
his foes lurked.

"Addison!" he snapped. "Round the corner, pronto!"

He shoved the bronc buster with his left hand, toward the turn of the building, and leaped after Addison. From the little rear window of Farney's quarters the shotgun flared, both barrels, and the spreading buck covered a large area as it shrieked through the night air.

"How bad's yore leg?" asked Hatfield. "Can yuh run a ways?"

"Yes, suh."

Addison was gasping, for his wind was gone. He had had a hard time of it, and the tear in the calf of his left leg was bleeding profusely, sloshing in his boot with every step. But the instinct to save his life, the excitement and fresh hope, kept him going as he fought off the shock of the injury.

"My hoss is 'bout three or four hundred yards east of here, near the end of the razor ridge," he said, his words jolting from him.

"We'll have to make it!" said Hatfield. "They'll soon be mounted and on our trail."

They darted around the front of the big store, the bulk of the building hiding them for precious moments. But they would have to dash across an open space, to reach the chaparral and Addison's horse, Blue.

A golden shape came galloping around the building, as Hatfield whistled again.

"Goldy! Here I am, boy!"

The sorrel, answering his human friend's signal, had jumped the corral gate, and come at full speed.

"He'll carry us double till we can pick up yore mustang, Addison," Hatfield said hurriedly. "Get aboard."

Hatfield boosted the bronc buster, whose injured leg gave way as he started to leap to the sorrel's back. Goldy's nostrils were flared, his eyes glowed. He lashed his tail, aware of the danger in the air. An angry shouting voice reached them.

"They went thataway! Spread out, shoot 'em down!"

Turk Monroe was outside, and Farney's stentorian tones came also.

"Hustle! Get your horses, boys!"

Chapter XII
In the Monte

Hatfield vaulted up behind Addison. There was no saddle, not even a hackamore on Goldy. Addison, however, was most expert as a rider, and Hatfield's long legs gripped the rounded ribs.

The Ranger could guide the sorrel with his knees, pressing gently with either one to indicate in which direction he wished to go, and Goldy would obey, although bareback riding, to a man used to the saddle was uncomfortable. However, thought Hatfield, it was easier than hanging around Big Bend and having Farney's gang work on him and Jerry Addison.

"Yuh got a wonderful hoss!" exclaimed Jerry.

"Goldy's the best there is!" Hatfield agreed.

The sorrel spurted along the road. He did not like carrying double but he had a fighting heart and would do whatever he believed

Hatfield wanted him to do.

The Ranger kept the store between them and the foe as long as he could, before cutting toward the shadowed ridges. Spurting guns flamed and he knew that the enemy had glimpsed them as they crossed the moonlit spaces. Bullets kicked up dust or shrieked close in the air, but they were streaking along. Hatfield fired once to drive the pursuers back and give them a few more seconds' time.

"Bear to the right," called Addison. "Blue's standin' in them thickets."

They entered the shield of chaparral and Goldy wove in and out, moving fast, avoiding the worst of the matted thorns and jumping holes in the sandy soil. Once he slipped, and nearly went down, but recovered and plunged on. The golden sorrel was beginning to breathe heavily. The weight of two men was a strain at such speed.

Soon they came to the spot where Jerry had left Blue, saddled, muzzled, his reins on the ground.

The bronc buster transferred to his own horse without touching earth. He leaned forward, snatched the bandanna from Blue's muzzle, and picked up his reins.

"Which way, mister?" asked Addison.

There was deep respect in his voice. After

all, just when he had figured his chips were all cashed in, the tall man, who could fight with such cold savagery, had shoved over a new stack.

"Reckon they've decided for us," replied Hatfield, jerking a thumb over his shoulder.

Addison glanced back. The dark shapes of Crimson Riders, already mounted, were careening across the open stretch, hot after them. The two ridges they were caught between forced Hatfield and Addison to pick one way, and that was east, along the trail below the heights.

Moonlight penetrated the cut, and the shadows were long and dense, but they were able to move at a good clip. Hatfield told Addison to go ahead while he watched for pursuit from the rear. From a cold start, Blue ran well. He was a beautiful horse, well-trained, and loved by Jerry Addison.

Watching how Addison rode and handled his mount, Hatfield felt real admiration, for the bronc buster was a genius at his profession. He seemed to be part of the animal he rode, and his ease in the saddle told how expert he was.

"Shore wish I had some leather between me'n you, Goldy," murmured the Ranger. "I got a hunch we'll be takin' quite a run."

Back at the carriage shed was his gear, his

saddle and bags, his poncho, all the equipment he usually carried. The necessity to save Addison from quick death had forced the Ranger to leave everything at Big Bend, but he did have Goldy.

"I can borrer a hull somewheres," he thought, "and pick up my stuff when I come back." For it was his full intention to come back, and soon.

The idea was to shake off Farney's killers, who were baying on his trail like a pack of wolves scenting blood. Wild bullets hunted him and Jerry Addison, but they had a start, and the long-legged, fine horses they rode gained yard after yard.

For two miles there was but the one way to move, and that was eastward with the Crimson Riders bunched behind them.

"Ridges peter out some not far ahead," sang out Addison. "Yuh want to turn? Say the word."

"Southward — that'll be best," replied the Ranger. "Thicker that way and we can catch our breath for a while."

The wind of speed whipped at the brim of his strapped Stetson. His gray-green eyes sheened in the moonlight as he looked back over a hunched shoulder. The Crimson Riders were still coming, but they had lost a good deal of distance.

Addison guided Blue through a gap in the ridge, which had lost altitude and fallen away. Beyond the gap a cattle trail made good enough going, and after a mile, they pulled up to give the horses a breathing spell and check on the pursuit.

"Think we'll make it?" Addison asked as he stood up in the stirrups to look back at the distances behind.

"We'll find out pronto," Jim Hatfield replied. "Keep down in the saddle."

Listening, they heard far-off hellos, and a gunshot.

"I believe they went straight on!" exclaimed Addison.

"Mebbe so. That turnoff wasn't too plain." Hatfield got down. He rolled a quirly, and squatted near Goldy to smoke. "How's yore leg, Addison?"

"It's still bleedin', but I'm all right."

"Let's have a look-see."

He helped the bronc buster pull off his boot, which was filled with blood. A nasty gash in the flesh, and two holes in the leather, showed how the bullet had ranged. With a strip of Addison's undershirt, the Ranger made a rough bandage to help check the bleeding.

"I don't know why yuh saved me, but yuh did, mister," said Jerry Addison.

He wanted to thank the tall stranger, shake his hand, and tell him how grateful he was, but it was difficult to frame the words. They sounded thin, beside what the bronc buster felt, and then, the big fellow did not seem to desire thanks.

"What's yore idea as to our next move?" asked Hatfield.

"I have some mighty good friends to the southwest, in Mariscal," replied Addison. He had squatted down, facing the Ranger. "And they're enemies of the Riders and Farney. I got a hunch Farney may attack 'em and I think they ought to be warned."

The Ranger's grim, rugged face was touched by a shaft of moonlight. He drew in a deep draught of smoke, his cigarette end glowing red.

"Mebbe so," he finally said. "But I'd like a word with K.O. Pierce, Addison. He holds a lot of influence in these parts, and that's what we need to beat Farney. We got to pick up plenty of fightin' guns to down the Crimson Riders."

Addison gave a deep sigh of relief. "I'm shore glad to hear yuh talkin' that way, Howes."

"Make it Hatfield — Jim Hatfield. I used Howes as a handle to fool Turk and Farney."

"Hatfield, then. I been tryin' to figger why yuh pulled me out of there at the risk of yore life. Yuh wouldn't have done it if yuh weren't a decent, brave hombre, that's a cinch. But — well, yuh rode with Turk and Farney and that fooled me. I would have bunched you with 'em if it hadn't been for tonight."

"I had a good reason for spyin' on the Crimson Riders," Hatfield said soberly. "But I couldn't let 'em finish you off. Yuh see, Jerry, I savvy more'n yuh think. I was with them cusses when they raided Mariscal that night. In fact, I was with Turk Monroe a couple nights before, while you were visitin' Contreras and the senorita.

"Turk has it in for yuh. He trailed yuh to Mariscal, meanin' to kill yuh, but the sight of that treasure caused him to change his plan. They figgered on stealin' the trinkets, and then Turk would catch up with you. A hound dog smelt us out when we were leavin', and Turk yelled we was from the KO, a lie to throw you and Contreras off the track. Do yuh remember the drygulcher's slug that near got yuh next day? That was Turk. We were lyin' up in that secret cave they got near Elephant Knob."

"Then you — then it was you who flashed that sun signal!"

"Right." Hatfield was pleased with Addison's perspicacity. "I'm tellin' yuh all this so yuh'll savvy I'm on yore side, with Luis Contreras and ranchers like K.O. Pierce. I aim to run them Crimson Riders into the slough and hogtie 'em. I can use yore help."

"Yuh got it, for what it's worth!" cried Addison. "I'm shore agin Farney and his gang. I got suspicious of 'em right off, when Turk tried to force me to join up. I found their cave, figgered they were usin' it as a hide-out. Then they hit Mariscal and stole Don Luis' belongin's, and I come to Big Bend to spy 'em out. Farney caught me."

It didn't take long for the two young men to set one another right as to what each had learned of the outlaw Crimson Riders. There was a strong bond between them, with the slim bronc buster naturally looking to the tall, imperturbable Ranger for guidance.

"How about Contreras?" inquired Hatfield. "Yuh reckon yuh could get him to furnish some fightin' *vaqueros* when we need 'em?"

"I'm shore I could," Jerry said eagerly. "The reason Contreras ain't fought before this is that he figgered it'd mean a terrible war between Pierce's bunch and the Mexicans, see? But once Farney's shown to be outlaw, and Pierce turns agin the Crimson Riders, Contreras'll fight."

"*Bueno.* Now, let's ride. Some of them skunks may sift this way."

They moved along narrow, winding trails made by animals, until they came out on open range, where they rode alongside one another. Addison's wound had stopped bleeding soon after Hatfield had bandaged it, but his leg was stiff.

As the new dawn came up, they were still many miles from Mariscal. The pursuit had driven them off the direct trail to the Mexican settlement. Hatfield's narrowed eyes swept the rolling, wild horizon. In the daylight they could be seen from afar, and careful as they were to pick the route, some dust rose from the hoofs of the horses.

The mountains loomed ahead, the shoulders forcing them into an ever narrowing channel in order to reach Mariscal without making a long, arduous detour. Hatfield didn't like it. At every hill, he would rise high on Goldy to peer around.

They rested the animals, had a smoke, and drank from a small water-hole. There were steers about, carrying the K O and other local brands. The sun was hot, nearly overhead, and the air dusty and dry.

Far off to the southwest loomed Elephant

Knob, and beyond that, on the trail south, lay Mariscal. The distances in the Big Bend country were breath-taking, long stretches without a sign of human habitation.

"Plenty of spots for an ambush along this trail," grumbled the Ranger. "Addison, I —"

He broke off, his Colt flying to his hand. They had come around a flat-topped hill, screened with mesquite and other thorned growth, and could see ahead for a half-mile. Half a dozen horsemen were on the road, blocking the way.

"Get back, Jerry!" Hatfield yelled, but it was too late.

They had been seen, and loud whoops, then gunshots, rang out. The sunlight glinted on metal badges, the Crimson Flower sign of Farney's killers. There were others than the mounted men ahead there, beating the bush. They came tearing up to join the men who had spied the Ranger and Addison.

"We're cut off!" exclaimed Addison.

"Farney must have started a gang straight off, last night, to watch for us down here!" said Ranger. "Careful! They got high-powered rifles."

A dozen or more of the Crimson Riders dug in their spurs, pulling up weapons to aim at the fugitives. They came galloping up the road, opening fire at long range.

"Let's head back for the K O!" cried Addison.

They turned their horses on a dime and fled before the furious Riders. But soon, as they took the trail toward Pierce's, they spied more enemies heading south, straight at them. To the east lay open range, which led into the brushy hills from whence they had come. Closer at hand, to the west, on their left, was broken country, and the Ranger swung Goldy toward it, followed by Addison.

"Lucky we give the hosses that rest," panted the Ranger.

Bullets hunted them, but they were moving fast and the range was long for accurate shooting. Hatfield saved his own lead. He had only what cartridges remained in his belts.

This time, shaking off the pursuers was not as easy as it had been in the darkness. Doggedly, the Crimson Riders, about twenty heavily armed gunnies, stuck to the trail of the fugitives. Up and down, through thick chaparral patches, dipping into gullies and crossing arroyos, Addison and the Ranger retreated before the Farney forces. From ridges, as they looked back, they could see the horsemen weaving on their trail.

The afternoon was gone before they eluded the enemy and paused to let the lathered, thorn-torn horses have a rest.

"They're between us and Mariscal," said Hatfield, as he smoked. "We can't warn the don now. If Farney wants to, he can hit the Mexicans, Jerry."

"He won't have as easy a time," growled Addison. "Contreras has more night guards out and they're ready if the Riders strike again."

"Well, I got a hunch that Farney's spread out his gang thin, tryin' to catch me'n you," Hatfield told the bronc buster. "He wants me worse'n he does you, for I savvy plenty, enough to make him and his bunch stretch hemp. First thing they got to do before they do any more raidin' is pick us up and put us out of the way. They'll kill us on sight. I reckon Farney'll let Mariscal wait till he's took care of us."

Addison nodded. "Yuh're right, Jim. I'm glad to hear you say it, too. What's yore idea — try to make the K O?"

"Yeah, it's the only place left. But we can't ride there straight off. If Farney has covered the Mariscal trail, then he'll have more of his gunnies around Pierce's. We'll move up as near as we can, and after it's good and dark, we'll try to sneak in."

"Suits me," said Jerry.

CHAPTER XIII
AT THE K O

It was rough going to the K O — that was, if they wished to stay off the open range, which the Crimson Riders were patrolling. Dark came and they moved out a bit, but the moon came up, and they had to ride warily, check every suspicious shadow so as not to run into an ambush.

Addison was familiar with the terrain, and he led the way after Hatfield told him what was desired. They ended up in some small hills only a quarter mile out from the big K O, Pierce's spread.

Low trees and brush offered shelter, and a spring, flowing in a small channel to the creek, provided water. They rubbed down Goldy and Blue, Addison taking the saddle off his horse so that the sweat would not burn the horse's hide under the leather.

"Yuh reckon yuh can walk the rest of the way in, Jerry?" asked the Ranger.

"Yeah, Jim, I'll make it." Addison could

put weight on his hurt leg although he limped as he tried it out.

"My idea is that Farney has the K O under watch," said Hatfield. "They'll see us shore if we ride up in the lights, but we can sneak in on the dark side and mebbe find Pierce."

"Bueno." Addison nodded.

He hobbled Blue so the gelding would not stray too far.

"That's right — make him comfortable," said Hatfield. He put an arm across the golden sorrel's arched neck, spoke to him in a low, soothing voice. "Stay here, Goldy, savvy? Yuh'll hear me whistle if I want yuh. If not, I'll be back."

Gently, he stamped the earth. Goldy sniffed, pawed at the dirt; perhaps he understood. At any rate, he had been trained to wait until Hatfield called him.

The horses cared for, Addison cached his saddle in a bush and prepared to follow Hatfield. They walked to the north down slope, and through the low trees could see the yellow rectangles of the big ranch-house's windows. There were lanterns hanging in the yard, near the corrals where night horses were held.

Addison gritted his teeth, as he limped along. It hurt to walk. He stayed as close as he could to the tall Ranger, who flitted ahead with the lithe, stealthy grace of a hunting panther. The Ranger circled until they were able to come in with the house between them and the rising moon.

"Wait, and I'll check up," he said in a low voice. "Take a breather."

The bronc buster was glad to lie flat for a few minutes to get his breath, and rest his leg.

Hatfield stole away, keeping low, skulking from shadow to shadow, with a rock here, a bush there, a contour of the ground serving to hide his form. The K O seemed to be normal enough. He did not see any saddled horses in the shafts of light around the house, and there were no riders circling the place.

Hatfield was pretty sure that Farney would have Pierce's ranch under surveillance but, as he had hoped, the spying scouts were posted some distance out, watching the in-trails. He also knew that Farney and Turk had spread their men out thin, in the desperate attempt to sweep up the tall man and Addison.

The front door was wide open, and by shifting his position, Hatfield was able to see K. O. Pierce, sitting in a chair by a round table, reading a newspaper. Pierce seemed to be alone in his main room. There would be cowboys in the bunkhouse, of course, and perhaps in other parts of the building.

"Looks like our chance," mused Hatfield.

He slipped back to pick up Jerry Addison.

They headed for a side door, on the dark side of the ranchhouse. Addison turned the knob, and stepped inside, with Hatfield at his heels.

"Howdy, K. O.," said Jerry Addison softly. "We've come back!"

Pierce nearly jumped as high as the ceiling as he left his chair. The copy of the Big Bend *Times,* which he had been perusing, fluttered to the floor. He turned, blinking his light-blue eyes. His bearded lips opened, forming words but for a time he made no sound.

Then he grunted, "Ugh! You might as well kill a man as scare him to death!"

Pierce had risen and stood with his big body tense. Bluff and hearty, K. O. Pierce was a real Texan. He was brave and fine, but he had a quick temper.

"I had a tough time, K. O.," Addison told him. "And we got a lot to tell yuh. This here is Jim Hatfield. He's all right, and I'll guarantee he's a man to ride the river with. He saved my neck last night, when Colonel

Farney and his gang was goin' to kill me."

Hatfield was watching the rancher's eyes. They were narrowed, and it was plain that Pierce was under a strain.

"Spooky as a wild colt!" decided the Ranger.

He let Jerry Addison start the ball rolling, as the bronc buster's words gushed from his lips, accusing the Crimson Riders.

"Farney and his bunch are outlaws, killers and thieves, Mr. Pierce!" declared Addison. "They fooled you cowmen into signin' up with 'em but they're no better — they're even worse — than Chihuahua Pete! They raided Mariscal and killed several men there, and robbed Don Luis Contreras. I trailed 'em to Big Bend, where they caught me and they'd have kilt me if Hatfield hadn't stepped in. He was hangin' out with the Riders, to spy on 'em and get information so's they could be arrested as they deserve!"

Breathless, Addison paused for a moment.

"Shucks," the Ranger thought disgustedly, "Pierce don't believe a word of it!"

The rancher stood stiffly. His pistol was in its holster, which hung from the back of a chair some feet away. K. O. Pierce was courageous, but he was no fool and would not dive for his gun if he thought he had no chance of getting to it in time. But he could not keep from flicking his eyes toward the weapon, as though hoping it might leap into his hand. He gulped, cleared his throat.

"I better get busy, I reckon," thought Hatfield, but a sharp command interrupted his intentions.

"Reach!" a hard voice said, from behind him. "Or we'll ventilate yuh both!"

Men bobbed up at the windows, while another bunch dashed upon the front porch and came through the door. They were K O punchers, armed with Colts and shotguns. One man, the wrangler, had even grabbed a pitchfork on his way over to the ranchhouse.

Hatfield had to make his decision quickly, in a breath of time. He might choose to whirl, draw his Colt, and fight, but he would surely die and all the targets he could see were cowpunchers, Pierce's own boys. He had come to help Pierce and the decent element in the country, not to gun them.

The stunned Addison licked his lips. His face went as red as a beet, but he slowly raised his hands, and looked over his shoulder. Hatfield followed suit. Behind them was a lanky cowboy, Roy Henderson, with a shotgun resting on the windowsill.

K. O. Pierce made a dive for his pistol and grabbed it out, cocked it, and covered

Addison and Hatfield. He gave an explosive sigh of relief.

"Whew! I thought I was cooked, boys!"

"Lucky I recognized Addison's voice, Boss," crowed Henderson. "I was in the next room, and I sneaked out and fetched the boys."

Pierce came up, and lifted Hatfield's pistols from the holsters, from behind. Addison was unarmed, for his guns had been taken from him by Farney's men at Big Bend. Hatfield, looking at the faces of the men swarming in, did not see any of the Crimson Riders, and he felt more hopeful.

"Look here, Pierce," he drawled, "yuh're makin' a big mistake. Addison and me are yore friends. Farney's Crimson Riders are yore enemies."

"Dry up, big feller," snapped Henderson, poking him in the small of the back with the shotgun.

"Jim's right, K. O.!" cried Addison angrily. "Are yuh plumb loco, actin' thisaway? We come to warn yuh!"

"Uh-huh," Pierce grinned. "Yuh could be parrots, sayin' just what Colonel Farney claimed yuh would. He told me what yore lyin' would sound like and he was right. Farney says yuh killed three men at Big Bend, when yuh was caught stealin' their hosses there. I'm s'prised at you, Addison. I thought better of yuh, but yuh made a fool out of me, hookin' up with this big hoss thief!" He scowled at the Ranger.

"Yuh're wrong, Pierce —" began Hatfield.

"Lock 'em up in the laundry, boys," interrupted Pierce, deaf to what the luckless pair had to say. "We'll send a rider over to Farney and let him know we've captured the skunks. I savvy all about yuh. Yuh began workin' with the Mexicans, Chihuahua Pete and Contreras, agin the ranchers on this range."

Pierce turned away, and cowboys nudged Hatfield and Addison to the rear of the ranchhouse.

The Ranger was chagrined. Farney had beaten them to Pierce, and K. O. was still believing in the Crimson Riders and their persuasive chief. Farney had guessed what they would tell Pierce and had anticipated them by informing Pierce, cooking up the yarn about horse stealing to explain the situation. So sure was Pierce of Farney, that he had scarcely listened to Addison and Hatfield.

Pierce lighted a lantern, and stepped to the low door of a small shack attached to one end of the kitchen. A pipe came through the three-foot-thick adobe wall, bringing water from a hillside spring. There was a drain in the stone-paved floor. Wooden benches stood along the walls, and there were some corrugated iron tubs, for washing clothing and blankets or to be used for bathing.

Big cakes of yellow soap stood on a shelf and the single room was dank, with the smell of wet wood and brick, and soapy clothing. There was a single window, but it wasn't wide enough for a man to snake through. The door was made of oak slabs.

"Yuh can stay here till they come for yuh," growled Pierce.

He drew back and slammed the door. They heard a padlock snap. It was dark, save for the little light which came under the door from the kitchen.

"Roy," they heard Pierce order, "put a guard on this door and another to watch the winder. They're mighty slippery customers."

"They'll slip on the soap if they try to sneak out of there," snickered a cowboy.

Hatfield sat down on a bench. "Here we are, Addison. I reckon we'll have to think this over."

"I — I can't believe it!" gasped Jerry. "To think Mr. Pierce would be in cahoots with Farney!"

160

"He ain't, really," said Hatfield. "But Farney's a mighty glib talker. He's beat us to the punch here. I should've figgered on that, before we walked in like a couple of school gals on a stroll! Yuh see, Farney has Pierce convinced. He's planted suspicion agin the Mexicans in Pierce's mind, and we ain't had the chance to prepare Pierce for the real facts."

"If they turn us over to Farney, we'll be shot as soon as we're out of sight of here, then!" Jerry said glumly.

"That's true. Once Farney takes us, we'll be gone geese!"

There was a pause. They caught the sound of beating hoofs, as a rider left the K O, headed toward Big Bend.

Pierce had sent the news of their arrest to Farney.

The hoofbeats of the messenger's horse faded away into silence.

CHAPTER XIV
DOUBTS

The two prisoners rested on a damp bench in the crude laundry room where they were locked in. The monotonous sound of the water running from the pipe and trickling away through the drain, was punctuated by noises from the bunkhouse, and the tread of booted feet. A man coughed outside the window — their guard. There were more of the K O crew in the lighted kitchen.

After a time, Hatfield rose and made a round of the room. Returning to Addison, he whispered:

"The earth's washed away some where the water's spilt over around the drain. Mebbe we better start diggin' — unless yuh'd rather sleep."

"I couldn't sleep to save my life," said Addison. "I'm plumb wore out but my eyes won't stick shut. I was a fool to fetch you here."

" 'Twas just as much my fault," said the

Ranger. "We do look mighty fierce, with all the dust and whiskers we've collected the last few hours. S'pose we amuse ourselves by playin' we're gophers? Make it quiet, so's the guards don't hear. I found a loose iron brace on that other bench. It'll make a good digger."

Addison detached a long spur from his boot heel and they began excavating. The sandy soil around the drain was easy to move. In an hour they had made a good-sized hole, and were well below the stone sill.

Then Pierce's booming voice in the kitchen caused Hatfield to stop his work. He put a warning hand on Jerry's arm.

"And give 'em some of them cold beans and beef and biscuits left from supper," the rancher was saying. "The cusses don't deserve no consideration but I hate to see even sidewinders go hungry."

Quickly, Hatfield covered the hole with one of the big washtubs, and pulled a bench around, on which Addison sat, hiding the disturbed earth. He washed up as well as he could at the pipe, wiping the grime from his face and hands on his shirt tail. Soon the padlock was undone and light came in from the kitchen lamp. Pierce and three cowboys were in the entry, holding plates of food.

"Here, stow this away," growled Pierce. "Farney ought to be here with his posse by noon tomorrer. He'll see yuh get what's comin' to yuh when he turns yuh over to the Law. Me, I figger that any hoss thief who gets as far as a trial is mighty lucky."

"Thanks, Pierce," said Hatfield calmly. "But how about it? Just give me five minutes of yore time. I can interest yuh."

"He'll sing yuh a siren song, Boss, and sell yuh a bunch of stolen hosses!" jested a cowboy.

Pierce was jumpy, just the way Jerry Addison was. The excitement had kept him from getting to sleep. He hesitated, as the tall man, who had a soft, persuasive voice and straight-looking eyes renewed his pleas.

"What harm can it do?" asked the Ranger. "I only want to put yuh on the right track. Are yuh man enough to listen, Pierce? I'd like to make it a talk between you and me — if you ain't afraid."

"Afraid!" cried K. O. belligerently. "Why, I ain't afraid of any man! Scat, boys. I'll talk to this smooth rascal if he thinks he can fool me."

The cowboys left the kitchen, although they didn't want to go. It was not so much that they didn't want to leave the rancher alone with the prisoners as it was that they were curious to hear what the tall captive was going to say, just as Pierce was. Hatfield stepped slowly out into the kitchen, blinking in the light. Pierce drew his six-shooter, keeping back so there was no chance for the prisoner to jump at him.

"I guarantee not to try any stunts while we're havin' our powwow, Pierce," Hatfield said earnestly.

K. O. Pierce patted his Colt. "So does this, big feller. Go on — talk fast. Yore five minutes has begun!"

"Well, what Addison told yuh is gospel, but yuh won't b'lieve that." And, in a soft voice Hatfield added, "I'm a Texas Ranger, Pierce, name of Jim Hatfield, from Cap'n McDowell's Austin headquarters. I come down here to clean up the mess yuh're in."

Pierce was staring into the level gray-green eyes.

"Huh!" he grunted at last. "I've heard that before, too, though Farney didn't tell me yuh would try to use it. Every cussed hoss thief yuh catch claims he's a range detective or somethin', playin' ring-around-a-rosie with the mustangs so's to trap the real thieves!" Then Pierce asked, "If yuh're a Ranger, let's see yore star."

"My badge is hid in Big Bend," said Hatfield, "where I went to work in with Farney and his Crimson Riders. I shore found out what was what, too. They're a bunch of outlaws. They've stirred up a fuss between Contreras and you, and they're runnin' a dirty game. Soon they'll strip yuh, mebbe finish yuh if yuh yell too loud. They aim to spread through Texas with this Crimson Rider business. They steal cows, turn 'em over to their confederates to sell for 'em, while they take yore money for protection!"

K. O. Pierce looked doubtful. He scratched his head, frowning.

"But Farney don't seem like a bandit," he finally said. "I'd have to have more proof than just yore word. Why, when we joined his Crimson Riders, Chihuahua Pete and his rustlers didn't dare hit us no more!"

"That was easy." The big man shrugged. "After stampedin' you ranchers into joinin' up with his society, Farney simply passed the word to his thieves to let yuh alone and steal from folks who refused to sign up!"

Hatfield had a certain magnetism, and a convincing manner that it was hard to resist.

"I wish yuh had yore badge with yuh," said Pierce.

"Why not send a couple of yore boys after it?" suggested the Ranger. "Have 'em pick it up on the q.t., though, or the Riders in Big Bend'll never let 'em come back. The way I figger is that Farney's gang are spread out at the moment, huntin' Addison and me, for we're dangerous witnesses agin 'em.

"They don't know I'm a Ranger. I had to leave Big Bend first, to save Addison, and I left my saddle and gear in that carriage shed. One evenin', when Blackie tried to search me in my sleep, I shoved my Ranger star under the sill of the shed. It ought to be there still, about four feet in from the back wall, the northeast corner."

K. O. Pierce licked his bearded lips. It was impossible not to be impressed by Hatfield.

"Now that yuh've washed yore face, yuh do look less like a hoss thief!" he admitted reluctantly. "Tell yuh what: I'll send Roy Henderson — he's a smart hombre — to Big Bend, and see if what yuh say about that Ranger star is true. If Roy finds it, we'll go on from there."

"Yuh can wire Cap'n Bill McDowell, in Austin."

"First I want to see that star," Pierce said flatly. "It's a long run to the telegraph office at the railroad station."

"Yuh've already sent word to Farney that yuh got us," Hatfield reminded the rancher. "Them Crimson Riders'll come a-ravenin' like a bunch of hydrophoby wolves!"

"When they show up, I'll take care of it,"

snapped Pierce. "Now, yuh've had more'n that five minutes. Get back in there."

Hatfield had accomplished something, sowing the seeds of doubt in K. O. Pierce's mind. He had been so certain of the integrity of Colonel Farney and his Crimson Riders, and when he had been furnished with "proof" that Addison and the big fellow were horse-thieves and killers, Pierce had only acted as any decent man would in such a situation.

The Ranger stepped back into the shed and Pierce locked them in.

"So yuh're a Texas Ranger!" whispered Addison.

"That's right, Jerry. . . . Come on, and let's see about that escape hole."

"But if K. O. gets too shore yuh're a lawman and that Farney's an outlaw," argued Addison, "he'll let us out."

"Shore he would. Provided he's still in control here. How many cowboys does Pierce hire?"

"Oh, twelve, fifteen, sometimes more in season. He's short-handed now, because the Mexican rustlers killed his brother, and a couple of his men took lead as well. There's one still lyin' wounded in the side bedroom."

"And Farney has sixty or seventy gunnies!" said Hatfield. "And Pierce has already sent word he has us. Farney'll take us if he has to wipe out the whole ranch. We know too much for him to take any chance of our gettin' away."

Addison hastily seized his loose spur and began to dig, and Hatfield squatted by him with the iron bar. They heard a rider leaving the yard.

"That'll be Roy Henderson, on his way to Big Bend," thought the Ranger.

The ranch began to quiet down. Usually the cowboys turned in early, except for those who must stand night guard on some herd collected outside the corrals. The prisoners in the laundry kept digging away, making a good-sized hole under the sill of the shed.

The sentry was sitting on the ground at the rear of the building, his back to the wall. The running water, with the restless stampings of stock in the pens behind the bunkhouse, helped cover the faint scratching sounds made by the two earnest workers in the shed.

But they did not have enough time. It had been late when they had reached the K O, and the hours had sped past. Soon a faint touch of gray showed, through the little window. The dawn was at hand.

The tiny rectangle had become altogether visible when they heard horsemen sweep in. Listening, they recognized Turk Monroe's harsh voice, singing out:

"Oh, Pierce! K. O. Pierce!"

"Hey, Monroe!" called a man from the kitchen. "Come here!"

Crouched by the door, Hatfield held the iron bar in his hand.

"I met yore messenger on the way to town," Turk was saying, at the kitchen entry. "Picked up a few of the boys — we was out huntin' them outlaws — and come arunnin'. Where's the prisoners? I'll take 'em right back to justice."

"Wait'll I call the boss," said the sentry.

Pierce entered the kitchen a few minutes later. "Howdy, Turk," he said. "Say, that bronc buster that used to work for me and the big hombre come here last night, savvy? I sent word right off to Farney that I had 'em locked up. And what yuh think! By Jupe, while most of us was sleepin', the big 'un played he was sick. When the boys opened the door, he snatched a Colt out of their holster and covered 'em! Then him and Addison stole a couple more hosses and escaped!"

"Pierce is a mighty glib liar," thought the listening Ranger. "If I wasn't stuck in here,

I'd almost believe him!"

He was greatly relieved, though, at the attitude of the rancher in refusing to turn them over to Monroe. That would have meant certain death. Turk would have shot Addison and him down, the moment they were away from the K O.

Turk Monroe was furious.

"What?" he howled. "Yuh mean to stand there and tell me yuh had them two lobos and let 'em slip through yore fingers? Why didn't yuh gun 'em?"

" 'Cause they proved too slick for us," replied Pierce. "Tell Farney if we come on 'em agin, we'll let him savvy right away."

There was a silence; then Monroe asked: "What's in there, Pierce? Yuh got the door locked."

"Oh, it's just a storeroom and laundry, that's all," the rancher said off-handedly. "Have some chow? We're goin' to eat pronto."

"No, thanks," said Turk dryly. "I've lost my appetite."

He was obviously much put out, and the locked door had aroused his suspicion. But K.O. Pierce was a determined man, and he had a number of cowpunchers close at hand who would obey him, fight for him.

"Tough luck, losin' them hoss thieves,"

drawled Monroe. "Well, Pierce, we'll be ridin'. Let us know if yuh get any more word on 'em."

"I shore will," Pierce said heartily.

The Crimson Riders left the yard.

"At least Pierce lied for us," Hatfield told Addison. "But I reckon Turk has gone to tell Farney and fetch a real crew after us."

A hot breakfast and a big pot of coffee were served the prisoners. They had the hole under the sill covered with the tubs, and there was no indication of what had been occupying their time during the night.

The day turned out to be a hot one. The sun beat down on the little shed, making it like a steam bath inside. The Ranger had dug as far as he dared for if anyone chanced to step on the thin layer of dirt alongside the adobe wall, a cave-in might result. The two captives stretched on benches and dozed.

It was afternoon when the Ranger, who slept on a hair-trigger, roused. Horsemen were in the yard, a number of them; he went to the little window and peeked out. Colonel Farney and some thirty Crimson Riders, among them Turk Monroe, were sitting their mustangs there.

K.O. Pierce, who had lost his night's sleep, was enjoying a siesta. One of his cowboys roused him, and he came out to talk with Farney near the back of the ranch house.

By straining his ears, Hatfield could hear the talk, brought on the warm wind. Farney was angry and spoke in loud tones, and Pierce soon grew heated at Farney's attitude.

"Turk says you had Addison and Howes," said Farney, "and that you let 'em escape, Pierce."

"I didn't let 'em," snapped the rancher. "They escaped by theirselves."

Hatfield waited. He had hoped that Roy Henderson might get back with the Ranger badge before Farney could collect his scattered forces and descend on the K O. But nothing had been heard from the waddy who had been sent to Big Bend for the star.

Farney was decidedly suspicious. His tone of voice and attitude proved that.

"Pierce," he said firmly, "you and I have been very good friends. My organization has given you protection against the rustlers. Yet now you permit two of the worst outlaws in Texas to get away, after you had your hands on 'em! How did they do it?"

"I told Turk," drawled Pierce. "Snatched a gun and run."

CHAPTER XV
SURROUNDED

Peering out of the little window beside which he stood, Hatfield could just see Pierce and Farney, Addison still asleep on his bench stirred restlessly and moaned in his dreams. The Ranger saw that the Chief of the Crimson Riders had dismounted to confer with the rancher.

"Farney's shore mad," thought Hatfield, "and don't believe what Pierce says!"

He could see the redness of Farney's face, and the violent twitching of the man's waxed mustache.

"The Crimson Flower organization," he heard Farney say sharply, "depends on co-operation, Pierce. Perhaps because Addison worked for you, you feel a certain loyalty toward him. That's a foolish attitude. As I proved to you Addison along with the big man, Howes, has stolen your horses. They're killers, and we have many witnesses to prove it. With my own eyes I saw them shoot down two men in cold blood at Big Bend! I want you to turn 'em over to me."

This angered Pierce. "Yuh mean yuh're callin' me a liar when I say they escaped, Farney?" he demanded.

Farney stared at the big cowman.

"Farney ain't shore of his ground now," Hatfield thought, "but he's afraid that somehow Addison and me have got Pierce on the prod."

It was a dangerous moment, as the two tall fellows faced one another, eyes flashing. Pierce's idea about Farney had been shaken, shaken by Hatfield's story. Farney, a clever rascal, realized it. And the Ranger knew that Farney was thinking now that if Pierce suspected him, there was only one thing for such a killer as Farney to do, and that was to dispose of Pierce. The K O owner had too much influence in the Big Bend country to permit him to spread the truth about the Crimson Riders.

When Farney spoke again, his voice was thick with restrained rage.

"Very well, Pierce," he said. "But you're still a member of the Crimson Flower. You contracted to remain so for at least one year, and to pay the dues and charges. Because of this mess with the two killers you've abetted, an extra levy must be made on all members. Your share will be five hundred dollars, to help defray the costs of the pursuit and pay damages."

"Yuh mean yuh want me to give yuh five hunderd dollars more?" growled Pierce, thrusting out his bearded jaw.

"If you desire to remain with us, yes."

"Shucks, Farney!" Pierce was thoroughly angry now. "I wouldn't give yuh a plugged nickel — not after the way yuh've acted today."

The warm air was tense as the two leaders eyed one another. Farney, in asking for more money, was needling Pierce.

Hatfield decided that Farney, certain now that Pierce suspected him, would kill the rancher as soon as possible. He gripped his iron bar. If a fight broke out in the yard, he might pry open the wooden door into the kitchen, snatch a gun from Pierce's rack, and start shooting, for the man who was supposed to be on guard in the kitchen now stepped outside to watch and listen to the argument.

But Colonel Farney was shrewd. He knew he would be the first target, if a scrap started then and there. Pierce had his gun in his holster, and he was fast enough to get Farney, if one of his cowboys didn't.

Without another word, Farney turned on

his spurred heels, leaped on his horse, and led his men from the yard.

K.O. Pierce was grinning as he walked to his stable. Farney and his bunch rode away, over the rise from the buildings.

Hatfield shook Jerry Addison awake, to tell him what had occurred.

"Soon as it's dark," said the Ranger, "we're goin' through our rathole."

"Bueno," said Jerry. "I feel a lot braver after that snooze. I was plumb wore out."

"Pierce is shook mighty bad," Hatfield told the bronc buster. "He's lost confidence in Farney. But he don't savvy yet what danger he's in. Farney won't leave. He'll hem in the ranch — see if he don't — and soon as he's fetched in his main force, he'll attack. I know his kind of onion. I'm mighty anxious for Pierce to throw in on our side. He can give us a lot of help in strikin' that gang of Farney's."

"Where yuh s'pose Roy Henderson is?" asked Addison.

"It prob'ly took him time to find my star, quiet-like. It's a question whether he'll be able to fetch it in, with the Crimson Riders guardin' the trails. And if they find that star on Henderson, there'll be thunderation to pay. Big thing is to collect all the help we can to fight Farney and his bunch. You sneak out, pick up Blue, and ride to Mariscal. Have Contreras furnish as many fightin' *vaqueros* as possible. Fetch 'em to the point where our hosses are, and I'll meet yuh there."

"Yuh're the doctor, Jim," agreed young Addison. "What you aim to do?"

"For the time bein', stick around here."

The cook was in the kitchen, banging his pots and pans, and cursing to himself as cooks are wont to do. Supper was on the iron stove, and the scents were appetizing. K.O. Pierce and his men were at the bunkhouse.

Dark fell over the great Big Bend country.

"Come and get it before I throw it way!" the cook bawled, and there was the usual stampede.

The men ate at board tables in a long shed on the other side of the house from the laundry annex which gave Jim Hatfield his chance. With his iron bar, he thrust through the few inches of earth crust left outside, and the hole was ready for them to go through it.

"Now, Jerry, you go over, tap on the winder, and talk to that sentry," ordered Hatfield.

Addison hurried to the end of the shack.

"Hey, Murphy!" he called, in a loud voice.

"When do we eat?"

Hatfield, in the darkness of the laundry, dived into the hole they had dug. The sandy soil was damp and the hole was a narrow fit for his wide shoulders. But he pushed his way through it and lightly drew himself up at the side of the shack. Addison and Murphy, the young wrangler, were talking, and the men eating in the dining shed were noisy.

The Ranger turned the corner. Murphy had his back to him as he peered in the window at Addison's dim face. An instant later, Hatfield had the slim wrangler, had choked off his cries with expert grip. He pulled the Colt from Murphy's holster.

"Take it easy, son," he advised. "I don't want to hurt yuh."

Murphy gasped, choked as he tried to squirm loose, but the tall Ranger held the young wrangler with ease until Addison, coming around through the hole, hustled up. A quick gag was put on Murphy's lips with his own bandanna. They tied his hands behind him and secured his ankles. Hatfield slung the wrangler over a shoulder, and carried the captive away from the house, to some bushes.

"Yuh get goin', Jerry," ordered the Ranger, "but watch out for Farney and the Riders."

"All right. Luck, Jim."

Addison limped, but the leg wound was healing and the shock had worn off. He could reach Blue, and ride for Mariscal.

"I hate to tie you up, Murph my boy, but I got to have it quiet for a while," said the Ranger softly to the wrangler, whose eyes rolled in the faint light. "I'll soon be back and leave yuh free."

He unbuckled Murphy's cartridge belt and strapped it on himself.

He made sure of the bonds and gag, and left Murphy in the bushes. He flitted toward the house, going around the front way, as the men of the K O were at the rear, eating the evening meal.

"I got to find a decent saddle," he thought. "And I got a Colt now." He had taken it from the wrangler.

As he reconnoitered, he saw a couple of men coming toward him. One was K.O. Pierce, and the other the lean Roy Henderson.

"I couldn't ride in, I tell yuh," Henderson was saying. "Had to sneak through the bushes after it got dark! I found that Ranger star right where he said it'd be, Boss!"

"Well, dog my hide," barked Pierce. "From the way Farney acted, I reckon Addison and that big feller wasn't lyin', after all! Give me his badge and I'll turn 'em loose. Farney got me so mixed up in my mind, I don't know whether I'm comin' or goin'.' "

Hatfield stepped out, went to meet the rancher.

"Saved yuh the trouble, K.O., and snaked ourselves out," he drawled. "Since yuh're shore now I'm who I say I am, let's get to work, for we've lost valuable time and Farney's on the prod."

Pierce stared at the tall, rugged officer. "I'm sorry I was such a dumfool," he said. "Here's yore star, mister."

Hatfield accepted the offering. As he was pinning it to his shirt something shrieked close, and smashed into the house wall, spattering them with fragments.

"Ow-w!" howled Pierce, jumping as he was stung in the cheek by a sharp bit of adobe brick.

"Let's shift," suggested the Ranger. "We're standin' right in the light of that winder, and it's too good a chance to miss. They'd like to down me and you, Pierce."

Hastily, Pierce led the way to the front porch. Hatfield had not forgotten the wrangler.

"Wait inside," he said, "but keep away from winders and doors. I had to tie up yore guard, Pierce, and I want to let him free. If yuh listen, yuh'll prob'ly hear some plain and fancy cussin' when I take off his gag."

He hurried to the spot where he had left the captive. As he reached the prostrate wrangler, who had been squirming around, trying to rub the cloth from his lips, Hatfield heard some bursts of gunfire from south of the buildings, down the creek.

"I hope they ain't shot Addison," he thought anxiously, for the firing had come from the direction of the wooded knoll where they had left their horses.

When he loosened the gag, the wrangler swore at him, and after he was freed, galloped to the house. When Hatfield entered the living room, the young fellow, his eyes wild, pointed at him.

"There he is, K.O.! He got my gun and done tied me up!"

"It's all right, son," growled Pierce. "Calm down. See that star?"

"A Ranger!" The wrangler gawked at the big fellow, awe in his youthful eyes.

"Here's yore hogleg," said Hatfield. "Keep it loaded. Yuh'll soon need it."

Hatfield held a hasty council of war.

"Farney's scared of you and me, Pierce," he said, "and he'll do his best to down us, for that's the only way he can hang on to what he's got. He's callin' in all his fighters and then he'll strike to wipe yuh out. Yuh ain't got but fifteen waddies or so, have yuh?"

"That's it." K.O. nodded.

"Farney can marshal four to five times that many Crimson Riders," Hatfield said soberly. "And if he sends for allies, it'll be worse . . . Have yuh ever heard of a wet cattle dealer whose handle is Lenihan?"

"Shore," said Pierce. "Must be Ike Lenihan. He's got a spread over near Presidio, but they do say he does some smugglin' and handles stolen cows back and forth across the Border. He's quite a drive from here, though, through the mountains."

"I believe Lenihan has drove off the steers stolen from this range, after Chihuahua Pete and Monroe rustled 'em," said the Ranger. "The Crimson Riders got a depot on the south side of Elephant Knob, and that's where Lenihan picks up the beefs."

Pierce thought it over. "Sounds logical," he said, and nodded again.

"Yuh better call yore boys together," advised Hatfield. "Warn 'em there may be an all-out attack any minute, and to be on the alert, guns loaded and plenty of spare ammunition handy. As to guns, I'd like to have my own back, and mebbe borrer a sawed-off shotgun."

"There's the rack," invited the rancher. "Help yorself, Ranger."

Pierce was completely under the big officer's spell now. He had turned from Farney, who had tricked him.

Hatfield stepped over and buckled on his belts which Pierce had hung on the racks after taking them from the Ranger and Jerry Addison when he had made them prisoner. Hatfield chose a fine shotgun, too, dropping spare shells for it into his pockets. Turning back to Pierce, he said:

"Now I feel dressed . . . But listen, Pierce. We're goin' to need help. How about your neighbors?"

"They'll send what they can," replied Pierce.

"Yuh'll never get riders through them gunnies out there," objected Henderson. "I seen 'em — I know."

"Yuh have a hoss hid in the monte, Roy," said the Ranger. "Could yuh snake back through their lines before it's light and ride to the next ranch?"

"I can try, Ranger," Roy Henderson told him. "Charlie Matson's place is a two-hour run from here — the nearest place — and he hires only eight or ten waddies."

"If yuh reach Matson's, have him send fast riders out to all Pierce's friends in this section," instructed the Ranger. "Collect what fighters yuh can, and fetch 'em to that thick grove of trees half a mile north of here on the crik, savvy? I'll get in touch with yuh there."

"I'll start right away," declared Henderson. He was weary from the long ride to Big Bend and back, but he was young and tough and devotion to his employer, K.O. Pierce spurred him to make the attempt.

But even as Henderson checked his Colt, and hitched up his leather chaps, preparing to leave on his dangerous mission, loud whoops and bursts of gunfire sounded about the ranch. Pierce's cowboys were yelling, and the heavy pounding of galloping hoofs shook the ground.

"They're comin', Pierce!" cried Hatfield. "Douse them lights, pronto!"

Chapter XVI
Siege

Everything was confusion for the first minutes of the rush. Lead whirled thick in the air, and Pierce's waddies, driven back by sheer force of numbers, retreated toward the buildings, as K.O., worried about his men, bawled instruction to them.

"Thisaway, boys! To the house, pronto!"

Hatfield, the shotgun over the sill, crouched at the corner of an open window which looked into the side yard. In the faint light he could see the K O men running in, could see the flash of pistols, carbines and shotguns aimed at them to cut them down. Riders swept through, dashing at crazy speed for the running men, circling the ranchhouse and shooting at doors and windows.

K.O. Pierce, frantic as he saw the men of his outfit about to be mowed down, kept yelling to the cowboys to get under cover. He opened fire on the fierce killers who were coming on in overwhelming numbers.

Hatfield let them get closer, and then blazed away with the shotgun. The buck spread, stinging the attackers and their mounts. One raider flew from his saddle and lay in the dust, but a couple of his companions paused long enough to pick him up and ride off with him.

"It ain't Farney's bunch!" howled K.O. Pierce, his bull voice rising over the din. "It's Chihuahua Pete and his rustlers!"

High-peaked sombreros were bobbing everywhere, and the faces of the raiders which could be seen were dark. The furious assailants wore short capes wrapped around their bodies, Mexican garb.

A mass of riders had swept around the bunkhouse and for a brief moment, Jim Hatfield had a glimpse of a man who must be Chihuahua Pete himself, a huge, burly figure in black leather, with a steeple hat trimmed with glinting silver tabs. The hat was cocked at a jaunty angle on his head, and from under the sweatband escaped flowing, tangled black hair.

It was the Ranger's first peek at the infamous and mysterious Mexican outlaw, and hastily the officer threw the reloaded shotgun around and let go with both barrels. But the bunch, with Chihuahua Pete in the middle, was moving at full gallop, and zigzagging. They were at some little distance, too, from the window where Hatfield was crouched, and buck spread fast. Chihuahua Pete, without being hit, whizzed past the corner of the ranchhouse, out of his sight.

"Shucks!" thought Hatfield. "Might've got him with a carbine."

Aloud, he shouted, joining in with Pierce: "This way, K O! Into the house! Hold the fort!"

K O cowboys were making for the doors or coming through open windows, singing out to their boss that they were here to fight.

"All right, boys!" bellowed Pierce. "Take the winders and drive the skunks off!"

Some semblance of order was obtained, as Pierce and the Ranger hurried around, checking up on the waddies. They began hitting some of the attackers, and as the ranchhouse blazed with defenders' guns, Chihuahua Pete and his *vaqueros* poured in a final volley and drew away.

In the darkened room, Pierce and the Ranger consulted.

"They'll keep us in here till they got enough men to take us," growled Pierce. "I don't believe Roy kin get through to bring help, Ranger."

"I'm willin' to make a stab at it," offered Henderson.

"We got to hold 'em back, till help comes," declared Hatfield. "My hoss is hid a short ways south of here, K.O. I'm purty shore I can reach him. When I whoop it up with the Rebel yell an yuh hear the shootin', Roy, then you make for yore horse, savvy?"

Hatfield made ready to leave. He took his Colts and, darkening his face and hands with charcoal from a burnt stick of wood at the kitchen stove, he offered Pierce instructions.

"Don't make any sallies, K.O. Stick to the house and gun 'em off. We'll start Roy — and Jerry Addison is well on his way to Mariscal. Don Luis Contreras'll send as many as he kin to help."

"Contreras!" exclaimed Pierce. "Why, he's in cahoots with Chihuahua Pete. I wouldn't be s'prised if there was some Mariscal *vaqueros* ridin' out there now!"

"That's another wrong idea yuh got to change, Pierce," Hatfield said sternly. "Farney used it to throw dirt in yore eyes. Yuh been so busy hatin' Contreras and his Mexicans in Mariscal that yuh was blind to what Farney and the Crimson Riders was up to. Contreras and his people are just as much Farney's victims as you are."

It was hard for the rancher to change his belief. But the tall Ranger had proved everything he said, so Pierce's objections weakened, and finally died down.

It was difficult to move about in spurred boots when trying to crawl and flit through the bushes, so the Ranger left his, putting on a pair of moccasins which Pierce fetched from his bedroom. He bound his black hair with a bandanna, so it would stay out of his eyes. A Stetson, too, was a nuisance when snaking along the ground.

Abandoning his cartridge belts, which might be noisy and betray his position, he shoved his pistols in his pants belt and wrapped some spare shells in a cloth so they would not clink together.

Dropping from a side window, he crouched on the shadowed side of the ranchhouse, peering into the night.

Flat on his stomach, the Ranger began his crawl, having picked out his first objective, the clump of bushes where he had left the wrangler. He made this and, peeking out on the other side, he could see the dark figures of horsemen in steeple sombreros, ranged in a rough circle about the ranch headquarters.

It was downhill to the creek, and the contours of the ground would help when moving that way. Some small trees and a few rock outcroppings would offer spots to reach and hide on the route. He decided to cross the stream and, once through the enemy line, he would circle and reach Goldy.

It took him half an hour to make the river bank, and when he reached it there were three riders not far away. But he froze until they had watered their horses and ridden off. Sliding down the sandy bank, the Ranger waded in the warm water, and made it up the opposite side. Here the chaparral was thicker, and he could lope along in his moccasins.

He had not said so to Pierce, for he wished to enhearten the defenders, but he was not sure that Jerry Addison had managed to win through. He remembered the firing he had heard not long after Addison had crept off, and it had been from the direction of the wooded knoll where the two had left Goldy and Blue.

But when he finally stood with the golden sorrel nuzzling his hand, he had seen nothing to indicate that Addison had been shot down. He went to the spot where Jerry had cached his saddle. The leather was gone, and Blue was not in sight. Of course, the Riders might have fired on the bronc buster after he had saddled up and was on his way to Mariscal, but he had at least been able to get a start.

"Have to do the best we can," he murmured to the sorrel.

Goldy was delighted to see him and showed it. He mounted bareback, and rode toward the flats, up the gentle slope from the creek, which curved around the hill.

Riders, dark of face and in steeple sombreros, were out there, watching the K O. Raising his Colt, Hatfield opened fire on them, and they swung to deal with him. Whooping it up with the shrill-pitched Rebel yell, the Ranger swept, zigzagging, across the rangeland.

Calls passed to comrades, and the sound of the shooting drew the attention of the killers. Hatfield made a tremendous hubbub, emptying his pistol at the foe, seeking to distract them, to pull them off so that Roy Henderson could snake through. The waddy *had* to make it, for time was passing and when daylight came, it would be impossible for messengers to sneak through the lines of armed men.

The Ranger rode hard, and the raiders pursued him. Once he whirled up a rise, and two of them thrust at him from either side. His Colt roared, and the killer on his right threw up both hands and flew from his saddle. The other one screamed and turned to flee as he felt the hot lead about his head.

The Ranger galloped on.

He had to shake them off, so he rode south, letting the golden sorrel show his speed. Goldy rapidly left the gunnies' mustangs behind, and before long Hatfield knew that he had done all he could to get Roy Henderson past the enemy lines.

Worn to a frazzle, the big Ranger decided that he must rest for a time. For ahead lay a hard, stiff battle. He reached the comparative safety of the dense chaparral a couple of miles south of the K O and, dismounting, curled up to snooze. . . .

It was dawn when he aroused. Horsemen were coming north on the trail to Pierce's, at full-speed. They were fine riders, and in moments Hatfield could see that they were *vaqueros.* In the new day, he could see their tall hats, then the dark faces of the Mexicans. But these *vaqueros* were friends, for they were led by Don Luis Contreras and Jerry Addison.

Hatfield leaped on the sorrel and trotted out to meet them, waving a greeting. Addison recognized him and Goldy, and quickly warned his Mexican comrades not to shoot as he swerved to meet Hatfield.

The Ranger counted thirty *vaqueros,* young and old, who had come from Mariscal. They were armed with pistols and rifles as well as with long knives.

Addison rushed ahead of them to shake Hatfield's hand.

"I made the best time I ever done, and the don come right away, Jim!" cried the bronc buster. "What's goin' on?"

"When I left, durin' the night," replied Hatfield, "they had Pierce holed up in his house. I figgered the K O could hold 'em off till we could make it."

"This is my friend, Ranger Hatfield, Don Luis," Addison said to Contreras. "The man I told you of."

Don Luis' face wrinkled in a smile, as he bowed.

"I am glad, senor! Ver-ee glad you hav' come to us!" Contreras wore a handsome outfit of velvet, with big leather flaps on his legs to ward off thorns. His black hat was of a flat-brimmed type worn by his kind. Fine pistols rode in his holsters and he had brought his shotgun along.

Addison had informed Contreras, as they had hurried north to aid K.O. Pierce, of all he had learned of Farney's perfidy.

Now that the Ranger knew that the Mexicans were on the way to aid the K O, however, he wanted to make sure that Pierce's other friends, his fellow ranchers, were ready, before he struck. Taking the lead with Don Luis and Addison, he led the band from Mariscal toward a hiding place from which they would be able to hear his signals. There he left them, and went on.

The sun was up, and warming, as Hatfield made his way on Goldy up the west side of the creek, hidden by stands of trees and brush. Reconnoitering, he could see figures in Mexican garb, all around the K O.

"Pierce is still holdin' out," he thought, with satisfaction.

He passed the ranch, a half mile to his right, and kept on up the river. Roy Henderson, with about twenty cowboys, hailed him as he slowed, looking for Pierce's messenger whom he had ordered to wait at this point.

"There's more a-comin', Ranger," reported the worn, bedraggled Henderson, who had been riding steadily for many long hours. "This is Matson's crew and some of Young's."

Gunfire had opened up from the K O. It grew heavier, and the smashing volleys smote the morning air.

"We won't wait any longer," declared the Ranger. "Let's go, gents! Sweep out in a half circle when we're in, and then push toward the buildin's. I got another force comin' in to pincer 'em from the south."

Topping a rise as he pounded toward the K O on his swift sorrel, Hatfield sighted the attacking gang. Urging them on to destroy Pierce and his cowboys, was Chihuahua Pete, his dark face framed by his curving sideburns and black beard. His hair flew wild in the wind of speed, and he was shooting in at the ranchhouse.

"Must be seventy of 'em!" figured the Ranger.

But Henderson had brought help from local ranchers, tough cowboys and their bosses, all good shots and first-class horsemen. With a score of such men at his back, the Ranger charged on. The signals he had arranged with Addison and Don Luis were spaced gunshots. But these would not be needed with the volleys to tell the Mexican contingent the raid was on.

Pierce and his men were firing from the windows. The Ranger drove on, riding bareback with an Indian's grace. He wore no hat, and his feet were cased in moccasins. But with his Colts, he was ready for the fray!

CHAPTER XVII
THE CHIEF

Riding at full-tilt, Hatfield galloped at the rough lines of the attackers, coming at them from their rear. His pistols roared, and the cowboys also opened up, cutting the enemy with their lead.

To the left, Hatfield sighted Chihuahua Pete's burly figure on a great gray horse. The Ranger, hoping to down the leader and so throw confusion into the rank-and-file of the rustlers, swerved toward the Mexican leader. Chihuahua Pete, howling and gesticulating to urge his followers to the fight, brought a bunching mob to meet the new threat posed by the cowboys. The raiding gunnies, seeing only a score of waddies charging in, believed they could overwhelm them.

Dark-faced riders in steeple hats and capes drove between Hatfield and Chihuahua Pete, and forced the Ranger to turn. The sorrel raced up the line, hoofs kicking up the dry dirt, mane and tail streaming in the wind. Low over Goldy, the Ranger fired at the foe, while their answering volleys kept bullets whistling dangerously near.

A lean enemy in a high-peaked sombrero and red suit, whose face gleamed black in the light, came streaking from the pack to cut off the swift sorrel. He rode like a crazy centaur.

"If he gits much closer, I can whirl and deal with him," thought Hatfield, and he held his fire.

He was clinging to Goldy's back with powerful legs, talking to the sorrel, guiding with his knees. The bony Mexican raider pounded after him, as Hatfield feigned to retreat, drawing him off.

"Cuss him, he's tryin' for my hoss!" the Ranger muttered angrily as Goldy jerked his head to avoid the slugs whining close around him.

Hatfield could tell by the angle of the pursuer's Colt that the man was aiming low, hoping to hit the golden sorrel's broadside. He pressed with his right knee, and Goldy turned on a dime.

At such whipping speed, it was difficult to take aim. The jolting of even the smoothest running horse made a poor stand from which to shoot, and besides the target was moving.

"Yi-yi-ki-yi!" shrilled the Ranger, the Rebel yell defiant in his pulsing throat.

From the other side of the ranch came an answering call, ringing on the breeze. It came from Jerry Addison and Don Luis Contreras, with their *vaqueros.* The Mexicans from Mariscal had spread out and were driving north, the east end of their line swinging around to sweep up the killers. Heavy blasts came from their pistols and carbines, and shotguns began to roar as they closed in.

Busy with his own particular opponent, who seemed bent upon running him down for the kill, Hatfield watched his chance. A slug seemed to cut his black hair which was tied back with his kerchief. He made a sudden turn again, and the lean outlaw after him had to veer and use both hands to control the gyrations of his horse.

Hatfield was almost upon the fellow as the Ranger reversed, the sorrel seeming to change ends in mid-air, so swift were Goldy's reactions to his rider's wishes. Colt up, hammer spur back under his thumb, Hatfield had a moment in which to take his aim before the bandit was able to bring his mount around so he could use his gun.

"I'll blow yuh wide open, yuh dirty spy!"

the black-faced gunman yelled.

Hatfield's thumb had risen, and he felt the comforting, sure recoil of his fine revolver against his palm. As he heard the cursing of his opponent, he realized suddenly that this was no Mexican rustler.

"Turk Monroe!" he shouted.

Close on the rider now, he could see the twisted, ugly mouth in the blackened face. He flashed by, and Turk's Colt blazed, but the muzzle of the gun was dropping. The Ranger lead had struck home. Turk sagged in his saddle, and when his mettled mustang whirled, his body was jerked from the leather and he crumpled up on the ground.

The Mariscal forces had clashed with the attackers of the K O, catching the gunnies in the rear. Henderson and the cowboys with him also were coming in, and when K.O. Pierce saw how things stood, he sallied from the ranchhouse, his men whooping it up.

The fight had become too much even for the attackers to stomach. Monroe was down, and they had seen him fall. They must have realized that they were done for.

Still, for brief but danger-fraught moments, the guns roared, and men clashed.

Then, with Hatfield directing the battle against the killers, they broke. They seemed to be leaderless. Chihuahua Pete was no longer in sight. The Ranger hunted for the huge rustler chief, but he did not see him.

The gunnies were running in all directions, every man for himself. Some rode for the creek, seeking to cross it and reach the chaparral. Others depended on the sheer speed of their horses, but other bunches were surrendering, caught between the pincering lines of the Mariscal *vaqueros* and the cowboys led by Pierce.

Hatfield, seeing that it was all over except for the clean-up, turned and rode back to the spot where Turk Monroe had fallen. He got down and squatted beside the dead man. Turk's face was stained black. He wore Mexican garments, but under his cape was his Crimson Rider badge, the red flower with the yellow center.

"So that's it!" muttered the Ranger. "But where's Colonel Farney?"

He had not seen the lean chief of the Crimson Riders since Farney had come to threaten K.O. Pierce.

"Hey, Ranger!" K.O. Pierce was shouting at him.

"Well, Turk," Hatfield murmured, "the joke's on you at last!"

He mounted, rode over to where Pierce, Addison and Luis Contreras were awaiting him. Cowboys and *vaqueros* had rounded up the bulk of the killers, and held them under guns.

" 'Twas a nice job," complimented Pierce. "What'll we do with all these prisoners?"

"The local Law can handle 'em, I reckon," drawled Hatfield. "They're the Crimson Riders, fixed up as Mexican rustlers! I got Monroe . . . Anybody seen Farney?"

Nobody had. Chihuahua Pete, too, had escaped.

Don Luis Contreras stared at Pierce. There was a stiffness between the two, for though both were fine men, they were leaders of different factions.

"Yuh have to thank Senor Contreras for hittin' 'em at the crucial moment Pierce," said the Ranger. "And I reckon you, Don Luis, are glad to see the Crimson Riders get what they had comin'. Yuh see, they were playin' you and Pierce agin one another, stealin' cattle and layin' it to the Mexicans in Mariscal, or at least sayin' you folks was hidin' the rustlers."

Contreras dismounted. He held out his slim hand to Pierce.

"Senor Pierce," he said, "I hav' weesh to be your friend!"

"The feelin's mutual!" growled Pierce, seizing the don's hand and pumping his

202

arm. "From now on, we stick together!"

Jerry Addison was grinning broadly as he saw his two friends shaking hands, and realized that the feud was over.

"Yuh shore done the trick, Jim," he said to Hatfield, in a low voice. "Say, where yuh goin' now?"

"To Big Bend, on the double, as soon as I can borrer a saddle and start. Yuh might collect a dozen fast-ridin' waddies and *vaqueros* and foller me, Jerry."

Colonel Bartholomew Farney ran out of the door of his quarters at Big Bend as the Ranger approached. A gray gelding stood outside the office, with two burlap bags slung over his back, to balance one another, and his lead rope on the ground. The colonel's saddled black horse with the single white stocking was waiting as well, his reins dropped. Both animals were fresh.

A bullet sang in the air over the Ranger as Farney swiftly mounted. It had come from one of the several Crimson Riders at Big Bend, guards who had been left to watch the place. Farney, however, was on his way. He believed that the Ranger was the advance guard of pursuers who would certainly catch up with him if he didn't leave Big Bend fast.

Goldy was dust-covered, damp from sweat, for he had made the run to town at a fast pace. Addison and his men were still some distance away, having been outdistanced by the golden sorrel.

Farney had a start. He turned and fired from the saddle with a long-barreled Colt, but the Ranger kept following, as the chief of the Crimson Riders picked up speed. With both his horses fresh he believed he could quickly leave the tired Goldy far behind.

"We'll never come up with him — not today," the Ranger thought.

He would not kill his beautiful gelding by forcing him to a death spurt.

"One chance," he murmured the next instant, and leaped from his leather.

He snatched the carbine he had borrowed at the K O and knelt, cool as he took careful aim at the fleeing Farney.

The first shot was to the left, for Farney veered from it slightly. The second, corrected by the expert marksman, sped on its way.

"Did I miss agin?" grunted the Ranger, for Farney had kept going.

Suddenly the tall renegade colonel slumped in his seat. His fine black horse ran on, but the rider slid off, a booted foot caught in the stirrup. The drag of the heavy body stopped the horse, and the pack-animal whose lead rope was tied to the saddle-horn, was brought up short.

Hatfield rode to the spot, gun up as he checked Farney to make sure the colonel was not playing possum. But he saw the bluish-red hole behind Farney's left ear. The carbine slug had penetrated to the evil brain, and Farney was dead.

The bags on the gray gelding contained the loot from Mariscal, and there were big rolls of bills in Farney's pockets. The chef of the Crimson Riders, knowing he was beaten, had tried to run for it. Farney's face gleamed in the sunlight.

Howls came from Big Bend. The guards had seen their chief go down, and they were staring at the Ranger. But riders were pounding into town now — Addison and his men. Guns spurted. The few Crimson Riders left at Big Bend turned to run.

Hatfield and Addison, after running the enemy out of the little settlement, went into Farney's headquarters. There were the maps, showing the operations of the Crimson Riders, as Farney had sought to take over Texas. In the sleeping-quarters, Hatfield picked up a padded black leather coat and thick black leather trousers. In a corner lay a black steeple sombrero, and a flowing black wig was nearby. A basin of water, soap, towels and rags showing black stains, were on the commode. A box of grease paints stood open on a chair.

"The dog!" growled Hatfield. "Farney was Chihuahua Pete! He fixed hisself up and rode with his men disguised as Mexicans, to fool the ranchers. That depot down by Elephant Knob was one of their secret camps, where they could change! That's why Farney's face always shone so. He had to scrub hard to rub all of the grease paint off his skin. . . ."

A week later, the big Ranger made his report at Captain McDowell's Austin headquarters.

"Yes, suh, Cap'n, this Farney had a bright idea to organize his Crimson Flower society and run Texas. He was makin' good progress, too, till we hit him. He started the feud between Mariscal and Pierce's faction, but that's settled. Jerry Addison, the bronc buster, is hitchin' up with Don Luis Contreras' purty daughter, Senorita Teresa.

"I laid a trap at Elephant Knob, where them killers had their depot, and caught a wet cattle dealer named Lenihan who'd been runnin' off the cows the Riders rustled, and sellin' 'em. But the beefs were only a sideline with them Crimson Flowers. It was the protective idea that Farney was makin' his real money at."

Many of the Crimson Riders had been arrested, Hatfield told McDowell, and the rest had fled. Peace had settled over the Big Bend.

But Texas was huge, teeming with life. In such a vast area there were always men whose evil ambitions posed a law problem.

Bill McDowell, his old eyes shining as he relived with Hatfield the exciting moments in the fight against Farney's Crimson Riders, swore, as he rattled a fresh sheaf of reports.

"Let's see, Hatfield. Down here, near the Nueces . . ."

A tame existence, the ways of the town, were not for Jim Hatfield. His nature craved the danger trails, the fight of the decent man against the bandit. He smiled, knowing what his Chief would say.

Later, McDowell watched him ride once more, carrying the Ranger word throughout the Lone Star State.

We hope you have enjoyed this Large Print book. Other Thorndike, Wheeler, and Chivers Press Large Print books are available at your library or directly from the publishers.

For information about current and upcoming titles, please call or write, without obligation, to:

Publisher
Thorndike Press
295 Kennedy Memorial Drive
Waterville, ME 04901
Tel. (800) 223-1244

or visit our Web site at:

http://gale.cengage.com/thorndike

OR

Chivers Large Print
published by BBC Audiobooks Ltd
St James House, The Square
Lower Bristol Road
Bath BA2 3SB
England
Tel. +44(0) 800 136919
email: bbcaudiobooks@bbc.co.uk
www.bbcaudiobooks.co.uk

All our Large Print titles are designed for easy reading, and all our books are made to last.